30/1/18

KT-493-480

This book should be returned/renewed by the latest date shown above. Overdue items incur charges which prevent self-service renewals. Please contact the library.

Wandsworth Libraries
24 hour Renewal Hotline
01159 293388
www.wandsworth.gov.uk   Wandsworth

The Life of an Unknown Man

Also by Andreï Makine

A Hero's Daughter
Confessions of a Lapsed Standard-Bearer
Once Upon the River Love
Le Testament Français
The Crime of Olga Arbyelina
Requiem for the East
A Life's Music
The Earth and Sky of Jacques Dorme
The Woman Who Waited
Human Love

Andreï Makine

The Life of an Unknown Man

Translated by Geoffrey Strachan

SCEPTRE

Originally published in 2009 as *u*
by Éditions du Seuil, 27 rue Jacob, Paris Cedex 06, France
This English edition published by Great Britain in 2010 by Sceptre

An imprint of Hodder & Stoughton
An Hachette UK company

1

A CIP catalogue record for this title is available from the British Library.

Hardback ISBN 978 0 340 99878 6
Trade Paperback ISBN 978 1 444 70975 9

Typeset in Sabon by
Palimpsest Book Production Limited,
Falkirk, Stirlingshire
Printed and bound in the UK by
CPI Mackays, Chatham ME5 8TD

Hodder & Stoughton policy is to use papers that are natural, renewable and
recyclable products and made from wood grown in sustainable forests. The
logging and manufacturing processes are expected to conform to the
environmental regulations of the country of origin.

Hodder & Stoughton Ltd
338 Euston Road
London NW1 3BH

www.hodder.co.uk

Translator's Note

Andreï Makine was born and brought up in Russia but *The Life of an Unknown Man*, like his other novels, was written in French. The book is set partly in Russia, partly in France and the author uses some Russian words in the French text which I have retained in this English translation. These include *shapka* (a fur hat or cap, often with earflaps), *dacha* (a country house or cottage, typically used as a second or holiday home), *izba* (a traditional wooden house built of logs) and *kolkhoznik* (a worker on a collective farm).

The text contains a number of references to streets and buildings in St Petersburg (formerly Leningrad) on the river Neva, including the famous Nevsky Prospekt, one of the main streets of the city's centre, Five Corners, the intersection of five streets on Zagorodny Prospekt, and Smolny, formerly the Smolny Institute, where the Russian Revolution started and which became the head-quarters of the Communist Party in Leningrad. The 'Scythian gold' alluded to in the text is among the trea-sures in the Hermitage Museum in St Petersburg. A boyar (in Russian *boyarin*) was a member of the aristocracy in Russia from the tenth century until the early eighteenth century, next in rank to a prince. In the performance of *Rigoletto* at the Leningrad Opera in 1945, referred to in the text, the central character is the King, as in Victor Hugo's original play, upon which the opera was based, rather than the Duke of Mantua, the change required by nineteenth-century Italian stage censorship and still generally observed.

Characters from French fiction referred to in the text include Rastignac, the character who appears in several of Balzac's novels, including *Père Goriot*, and Michel Strogoff, the eponymous hero of a novel by Jules Verne. Prince Myshkin is the central character in Dostoevsky's novel *The Idiot*. E. M. Cioran, the Romanian writer, who died in Paris in 1995, was known for his pessimistic philosophy expressed in aphorisms. The Latin text quoted on page 16 is from Catullus and may be translated as 'she who was loved by me as none will ever be loved'.

I am indebted to a number of people, including the author, for advice, assistance and encouragement in the preparation of this translation. To all of them my thanks are due, notably Giles Barber, Ann and Christopher Betts, Thompson Bradley, Edward Braun, Amber Burlinson, Robert Caston, Ludmilla Checkley, Daphne Clark, Bruce Crisp, June Elks, Will Fyans, Scott Grant, Martyn Haxworth, Wayne Holloway, Russell Ingham, Catherine Merridale, Geoffrey Pogson, Pierre Sciama, Simon Strachan, Susan Strachan and, above all, my editor at Sceptre, Carole Welch.

G.S.

I

One evening they amused themselves by hurtling down a snow-covered hill on a toboggan. The cold lashed them in the face, a fine cloud of hoar frost blurred their vision and at the most thrilling moment of the descent, the young man seated behind her whispered: 'I love you, Nadenka.' Mingled with the whistling of the wind and the loud roar of the runners, his murmured remark was barely audible. A declaration? The gusting of the snow flurry? Panting, their hearts laid bare, they climbed back up the slope, plunged into a fresh descent and again that whisper, more discreet still, spoke of a love borne swiftly away on the tempest of white. I love you, Nadenka . . .

'Bloody Chekhov! In his day you could still write like that.' Shutov pictures the scene: heady cold, the two timid lovers . . . Nowadays they'd say it was over the top. They'd mock it as 'sentimental rubbish'. Hopelessly old fashioned. And yet it works! He judges it as a writer. Chekhov's touch is there: yes, the deadpan way he has of rescuing a subject anyone else would have drenched in sugary sentiment.

That: 'I love you, Nadenka,' under cover of whirling snowflakes. It works.

He smiles wryly, used to being wary of his own

3

enthusiasms. 'It works all right, thanks to this bottle of whisky,' he tells himself, replenishing his glass. And also thanks to his lonely existence in this flat, where one of the occupants is a now absent young woman, Léa, who's coming tomorrow to collect her things, a pile of cardboard boxes beside the door. A tombstone that puts paid to any hope of love.

He pulls himself together, dreading the self-indulgent gloom that has dogged him for months. Lonely existence? A fine cliché! Paris is a city of loners . . . unless you're Hemingway painting the town red in the twenties. No, Chekhov's little device works because of the way his story slips forward in time: the two lovers part, settle down, have children, then meet again twenty years later in the same park and laughingly board a toboggan. And it happens all over again: the snowy breeze, the gleeful panic as they twist and turn, the strident screaming of the runners . . . As they reach top speed the woman hears: 'I love you, Nadenka . . .' but this murmur is no more than a distant music, protecting the secret of her youthful love.

So simple, yes, and yet so right, so evocative! They could still write like that in the good old days. No Freud, no post-modernism, no sex in every other sentence. And no worrying about what some little idiot with slicked-back hair on a television chat show will say about it. Which is why it still stands up. These days you have to write differently . . .

Shutov gets up, staggers, stoops over Léa's things, picks up a book, opens it at random, gives a dry laugh. '. . . The scent of roses? Forget it. What passes from the mistress's mouth to her lover's is saliva, along with a whole army of germs. It passes from the lover to his wife, from the wife to her baby, from the baby to its aunt, from the aunt, a waitress in a restaurant, to a customer whose soup she has spat in, from the customer to his wife, from the wife to her lover and thence to other mouths, so that every one of us is immersed in an ocean of intermingled saliva that binds us into a single common-wealth of saliva, a single moist, united humanity.'

Revolting . . . And it constitutes an entire credo. Formu-lated by a writer whom Léa idolizes and whom Shutov regards as drearily pretentious. A far cry from Chekhov. Nowadays a hero has to be neurotic, cynical, impatient to share his unsavoury obsessions with us. Because his trouble is that his mother still has him on a leash even when he makes love. That was how Léa's idol talked.

'If I'd known my mother,' reflects Shutov, 'I'd have spoken about her in my books.' The thought revives in him the oldest memory of his life. A child sees a door closing: without knowing who it is that has just left, he senses it is someone he loves with all his tiny, still mute being.

Beyond the window pane, a May night, the fantastical collection of ancient facades marching up the slope of Ménilmontant. How often had he longed to talk to Léa about these moonlit rooftops! As if covered in snow. He had found no image to capture the poetry of this sleeping whiteness. Rooftops made nacreous by the moon? No, that's not it. In any case, what's the point of trying to find an evocative phrase? Léa has gone and this 'dovecote' (which was what she used to call the converted attic) has reverted to being one of those oddly shaped dwellings that estate agents advertise under the ambiguous heading: 'Unusual property'. Shutov's face twists into a grimace. 'That's probably how they regard me. Unusual . . .'

And yet . . . He is the absolute prototype of a man ditched by a woman young enough to be his daughter. The plot for a lightweight novel in the French manner, a hundred pages of Parisian bed-hopping and gloom. All a love affair such as his would be worth.

He crouches down in the corner where Léa's things are piled up. 'You're not a failure,' she told him one day. 'No. You're not even embittered. Not like one of those East Europeans, people like Cioran and the rest. You're just unlucky. Like someone . . . like someone who . . .' (she was searching for the word and he was wild with gratitude: she's understood me, I'm not a professional failure!) – 'That's it. You're like an un-detonated shell with its devastating power intact. You're an explosion still waiting to be heard.'

In all his life no one had spoken to him like that. He had lived to the age of fifty, done a great deal of reading and study, experienced poverty and fleeting success, gone to war and come close to death, but it had taken a young Frenchwoman to explain to him what other people regarded as a wasted life. 'An explosion still waiting to be heard . . .' Which, in fact, is the common fate of all true artists. Very intelligent, that girl. Dear, good Léa. 'My Léa . . .'

Or else, maybe just a bitch who made use of this dovecote while she had nowhere else to stay and who's going off now because she's found herself a 'guy' who'll give her a roof over her head. A young 'babe' setting out to conquer Paris, leaving Shutov to rot, an old madman obsessed with his search for an epithet to describe that lunar whiteness on the rooftops.

'I love you, Nadenka . . .' He pours himself another whisky, downs it with the grimace of one who has seen through the universal grubbiness of human nature, but at the same time, with a writer's reflex, observes himself and finds his own posture false and exaggerated. No, there's no point in doing a bitter little Cioran number of his own. For whose benefit, in any case? Freed of the mask of disgust, his face softens, his eyes mist over. 'I love you, Nadenka . . .' If that story still works, Shutov tells himself, it's because I once knew a love like that. And that was . . . yes, more than thirty years ago.

Except that it happened not in winter but beneath the translucent gold of autumn. The start of his studies in Leningrad, a feminine presence along pathways re-dolent of the acrid tang of dead leaves. A girl of whom the only trace now is a tenuous silhouette, the echo of a voice . . .

The telephone rings. Shutov struggles out of the sofa's depths, stands – a drunken sailor on a ship's deck. The hope of hearing Léa sobers him up. His racing thoughts imagine a combination of excuses and back-pedalling, which might enable them to get together again. He lifts the receiver, hears a dialling tone and then, on the other

7

side of the wall, a vibrant male voice: his neighbour, an Australian student, whom his Antipodean friends often telephone during the night. Since Léa's departure Shutov's ear is constantly cocked (telephone, footsteps on the stairs) and there is little sound insulation in his attic. His neighbour laughs with frank, healthy candour. To be a young Australian with fine, white teeth, living amid the rooftops of Paris. Bliss!

Before sinking back into the depths of the sofa he wanders round to the corner where Léa's cardboard boxes are stacked. There is a bag of her clothes as well. The silk blouse he gave her . . . One day they bathed in the sea, near Cassis; she got dressed and when she tossed her hair back in a swift movement to tie it up, her wet locks made a pattern of arabesques on the silk . . . He has forgotten nothing, the fool. And these memories tear at his guts. No, at his eyelids, rather (make a note: the pain rips away your eyelids, making it impossible to banish the vision of the woman who has left you).

Damn those eyelids! Always his scribbler's mania. The conclusion is simpler than that: a young woman who breaks up with an ageing man should never leave him alive. That's the truth! Léa should have knifed him, poisoned him, pushed him off that old stone bridge in the Alpine village they visited one day. It would have been less inhuman than what she did. Less tormenting than the sleek softness of this silk. Yes, she should have killed him.

Which, in fact, is more or less what did happen.

*   *   *

8

Shutov remembers clearly the precise moment when the execution took place.

They often used to argue but with the theatrical violence of lovers, aware that the fiercest tirades will fade away at the first moans of pleasure. Shutov would rage against the poverty of contemporary literature. Léa would drum up a whole army of 'living classics' to contradict him. He would thunder against writers castrated by political correctness. She would quote what she called a 'brilliant' passage. (It was, among other things, about a son held on a leash mentally by his mother while he makes love to a woman.) They would loathe one another and, half an hour later, adore one another and what was really important was the glow from the sunset coming in through the skylight, gilding Léa's skin and heightening a long scar on Shutov's shoulder.

For a long while he turned a blind eye. The tone of their arguments changed: Léa becoming less combative, he more virulent. He sensed a threat in this indifference and was now the only one still ranting and raving. Especially that evening when he had received one of his manuscripts back, rejected. That was when, picking her way between words, she had compared him to an explosion unable to make itself heard . . . After they had split up Shutov would come to perceive that this had been the last flush of tenderness within her.

Then the dismantling began (beneath the windows of his attic, workmen were removing some scaffolding: yet another stupid parallel, the writer's mania) and their union was taken apart as well, a storey at a time. Léa came increasingly rarely to the dovecote, explaining her

9

absences less and less, yawning and letting him shout himself hoarse.

'The awesome power of a woman no longer in love,' thought Shutov, peering at himself in the mirror, feeling the crow's feet around his eyes, promising to be more conciliatory, a little more devious about his own convictions, to come to terms with her 'living classics' . . . Then took to shouting again, invoking the sacred fire of the poets. In short, making himself unbearable. For he was in love.

The assassination took place in a café. For ten minutes or so, Shutov made an effort to be nice, *gentil*, as the French say, then, unable to hold back, erupted ('an explosion!' he thought later, mocking himself). Everything came under fire: the wheeling and dealing of the book world, the fawning wordsmiths who suck up to the hoi polloi as well as the chattering classes, Léa herself ('The truth is you're just a groupie to that rotten little elite'); even the newspaper poking out of her bag. ('Go ahead! Lick the boots of your "Prosecco socialists". Maybe they'll take you on as a stringer for their *Paris Pravda*.') . . . He felt ridiculous, knowing there was only one thing he should be asking her: do you still love me or not? But he dreaded her reply and clung to the memory of their arguments in the old days, which used to founder, lovingly, in an embrace.

At first Léa succeeded in passing off the scene to the other customers in the café as a somewhat lively but amicable squabble. Then came the moment when the acrimonious tone was no longer fooling anyone: a middle-aged gentleman was tearing a strip off his girlfriend, who was, incidentally, far too young for him. Léa felt trapped. Get up and walk away? But she still had quite a lot of stuff to collect from this madman's attic and he was capable of throwing it all out into the street. Shutov would never know if such thoughts passed through her mind. Léa's face hardened. And with a bored expression she aimed her blow where she knew him to be defenceless.

'By the way, I've learned what your surname means in Russian . . .' she announced, taking advantage of the umpteenth coffee he was downing with a grimace.

Shutov pretended surprise but his face took on an evasive, almost guilty expression. He stammered: 'Well, you know . . . There are several possible derivations . . .'

Léa emitted a peal of laughter, a tinkling cascade of breaking glass. 'No. Your name has only one meaning . . .' She kept him waiting, then in a firm, disdainful voice, let fly: '"*Shut*" means "clown". You know – a buffoon.'

She got up and made her way to the exit without hurrying, so confident was she of the effect of her words. Stunned, Shutov watched her walking away, followed by amused glances from the other customers, then jumped up, ran to the door and there, amid the passers-by, yelled out in a voice whose pained tones astonished even himself: '*Shut* means a sad clown! Remember that! And this sad clown loved you . . .'

The end of the sentence faded away into a cough. 'Like the whispering of the young lover in Chekhov's story,' it occurred to him one evening, as he was staring at the last of Léa's cardboard boxes, stacked there in the corner of the dovecote.

But that day, on his return from the café, for a long time he was incapable of thought, once more picturing a child in a row of other children, all dressed the same, a boy taking a step forward on hearing his name called and shouting: 'Present,' then resuming his place. They are lined up in front of the grey orphanage building and after the roll call they climb into a lorry and go off to work amid muddy fields under a fine hail of icy tears. For the first time in his life the child perceives that this name, Shutov, is his only possession here on this earth, the only thing that makes him 'present' in other people's eyes. A name he will always feel slightly ashamed of (that damned derivation!) but to which, however, he will be attached, for it is the name borne by that still mute little being who had seen the door closing on the person he loved most in all the world.

Across the street from the dovecote there is a narrow building with faded walls ('it's been out in the sun too long, it's peeling,' Léa used to say). The moon moves bit by bit across the little top-floor flat. The workmen have not closed the windows and the room shines, like a sleepwalker's dream. An old woman had lived there once, then disappeared, dead no doubt; the dividing walls have been demolished to make an open-plan studio, as fashion dictates, and now the moon keeps watch over this empty space and a drunkard with sad eyes marvels at it, as he whispers words intended for the woman who will never hear him.

After making love with her 'guy', she is asleep now in their new 'space' . . .

And everything hurts him, the way he imagines Léa's friends talking and the idea of that young body, so close to him yet irretrievably lost. A body as supple as a frond of seaweed which, in their intimacy, retained a touching, vulnerable awkwardness. To be dispossessed of those feminine arms, of those thighs, of Léa's night-time breathing: the mere thought of it is a blow to his solar plexus. A crude jealousy, a feeling of amputation. It will pass, Shutov knows this from experience. A body desired that now gives itself to another man can be

13

forgotten quickly enough. More quickly, even, than one's regret at never having spoken of the moon passing over the flat across the street, of the woman who lived there, suffered, loved. And of the new life that will fill this white shell, bring in furniture, prepare meals, love, suffer, hope.

On occasion, after their literary quarrels, after making love, they would reflect on such unsettling aspects of human life. At these moments Shutov always felt that this was how he would have liked to be: passionate but detached, sensual and at the same time conscious that, thanks to their measured conversations, Léa was rising with him to glorious heights . . .

A window lights up on the third floor of the building opposite. A young man, naked, opens a refrigerator, takes out a bottle of mineral water, drinks. A young woman, naked as well, goes up to him, embraces him, he moves away, his mouth clamped to the neck of the bottle, splutters, sprays his girlfriend, they laugh. The light goes out.

'That could be Léa with her boyfriend,' thinks Shutov and, curiously enough, the scene eases the pangs of jealousy in the pit of his stomach. 'They're young. What do you expect . . . ?'

He moves away from the window, collapses onto the sofa. Yes, his fatal error was to complicate everything. 'She was rising with me to glorious heights . . .' What bollocks! A man unhappily close to the age of fifty suddenly has the luck to meet a pretty young woman who is no fool. And genuinely fond of him. He ought to take wing with joy, soaring aloft like a paraglider. Sing, bless heaven. And, above all, make the most of

14

it. In the greediest sense of the phrase. Make the most of her clumsy because genuine tenderness, of their excursions ('We're off to Paris,' they would say, travelling down from their patch in Ménilmontant), of the whispering of the rain on the roof at night. Of all those clichés of a love affair in Paris (oh, that singing of the rain!), intolerable in a book but so sweet in real life. Of this remake of a sixties romantic comedy . . .

For their love did last two and a half years, after all. Which is a good deal longer than an affair in one of today's novels. He could very well have lived out one of those little stories that crowd the bookshop shelves: two characters meet, fall in love, laugh, weep, part, are reunited, and then she leaves or kills herself (according to taste) while he, with a tormented but handsome face, drives away into the night along an *autoroute*, heading for Paris, for oblivion. They were both of them in good health, as it happened, and with no suicidal tendencies. And, as for *autoroutes*, Shutov avoided them, not being a very confident driver. Yes, he could quite simply have been happy.

To achieve this, he should have risked being clear from the start: a young woman from the provinces leaves her parents, or rather her one-parent family, based in an economically deprived region to the north of the Ardennes, arrives in Paris where she runs into an 'unusual' man who can give her a roof over her head. The young woman dreams of writing ('like all the French,' thinks Shutov) and although he is a writer with a limited readership, he will give her advice, possibly even help her to get published.

15

That, objectively, was their situation. All Shutov had to do was to accept it . . . But, like so many Russians, he believed that a happiness derived from petty practical arrangements was unworthy of people in love. At the age of fourteen he had read a story by Chekhov in which a couple's material well-being counted for nothing beside the heady thrill of a moment on a snow-covered hill, on a toboggan run. At the age of eighteen he had spent weeks strolling up and down in Leningrad's parks beneath a golden canopy of foliage in the company of a girl: more than a quarter of a century later he would remember this as a vitally important time in his life. At twenty-two, as a young soldier sent to Afghanistan, he had seen an old woman lying dead in the courtyard of a house, clutching her dog in her arms, both of them killed by an exploding shell. Noticing his tears, his regimental comrades had called him a wimp (several years later this choking back of a sob would lead him on to political dissidence . . .) From his university studies he would retain the memory of a Latin text, words that had inspired Dante: '*Amata nobis quantum amabitur nulla.*' He meditated long on a woman 'loved as none will ever be loved'. Such a love called for a sacred language. Not necessarily Latin, but one that would elevate the beloved above the mundane. *Amata nobis* . . . I love you, Nadenka . . .

Shutov stirs, woken by a dull cry escaping from his own throat which was pressed against a cushion on the sofa. The drink tastes like a dentist's local anaesthetic.

16

A useless swig, it would take three or four like that for him to reach a level of drunkenness that would turn Léa's cardboard boxes into inoffensive, swaying, unreal blurs . . .

Unreal . . . That says it all! Asking a flesh and blood woman to be a dream. Imagine living with a madman who thinks you capable of walking on a moonbeam! He had idealized her from the first moment. Yes, from the first words they had exchanged on a Sunday evening, one as dreary as any wet February night in the chilly station hall at the Gare de l'Est . . .

They were telephoning from adjacent cabins, two telephones separated by a sheet of glass, in fact. She (he would later learn) was ringing a vague acquaintance who had promised to put her up. He was trying to catch a publisher at home (on his return from his luxury villa in Normandy, purchased, Shutov reflected ironically, from the proceeds of publishing pulp fiction). Suddenly the girl turned round, a phonecard in her hand, and he heard a whispered exclamation that was both frantic and amused. Cheerful astonishment, on the brink of tears. 'Oh shit! The credit's run out . . .' Adding in a louder voice: 'And now I've had it!' Shutov had not caught her eye; at first she did not realize he was offering her his card. (The publisher's wife had just put him in his place. 'I've told you already. Ring him tomorrow at the off . . .' Proudly, he hung up on her.) Léa thanked him, dialled the number again. Her girl-friend could not put her up, because . . . She hung up as well, but slowly and indecisively, slipped the card into her wallet, murmured goodnight and wandered

17

over to the timetable screen. Shutov hesitated between versions in different languages. In Russian, word for word, it would be: 'And my card, young woman?' In French: 'Mademoiselle, may I have my card back?' No. Perhaps: 'Hey, you! Aren't you going to . . .' Not that either. Well, in any event, he was too old for the retrieval of a phonecard to cause more than a moment of embarrassment . . .

He strolled away thinking about an opening for a story in the style of André Maurois: a woman walks off with the phonecard a man has just lent her . . . What next? Every time she walks past that telephone booth she thinks of him? No, too Proustian. Better: a foreigner (himself, Shutov) runs after the woman to get his card back, calling out in his appalling accent; the woman thinks she's being attacked and sprays him with tear gas (alternatively: lays him out with a stun gun) . . .

He had already got a good way up the Boulevard Magenta when a breathless voice called out to him, then a hand touched his elbow. 'I'm so sorry. I went off with your card . . .'

He fell in love with every aspect of Léa. Everything about her that caught his eye had the completeness of a sentence that needs no rewriting. Her old leather jacket with its threadbare lining, a tight-fitting jacket which had ended up being moulded to the curves of Léa's body. Even when it hung on the back of the door at the dovecote this garment retained the imprint of her contours. And then Léa's notebooks, the slightly

18

childish diligence of her writings; 'very French,' Shutov told himself, perceiving in them the obsessive search for the elegant phrase. And yet the mere sight of these notebooks now seemed vital. As did the frozen gesture that for him was a poem in itself: an arm flung far out across the covers by Léa in her sleep. That slender arm, a hand with fingers that trembled from time to time, in response to the secrets of some dream. A beauty independent of her body, of the attic awash with moonlight, of the outside world.

Yes, that had been his mistake, his desire to love Léa as one loves a poem. It was to her that he read Chekhov's story one evening: two irresolute lovers, their meeting twenty years later. I love you, Nadenka . . .

'An exile's only country is his country's literature.' Who said that? Shutov cannot place the name in his confused thoughts. Some anonymous expatriate, no doubt, waking in the night and trying to recall the last line of a rhyme learned in childhood.

For a long time he had lived in the company of the faithful ghosts that are the creatures brought into being by writers. Shadowy figures, certainly, but in his Parisian exile he got on well with them. On a fine summer's day in Moscow, Tolstoy saw the figure of a woman through an open window, a bare shoulder, an arm with very white skin. All of Anna Karenina was born, if we are to believe him, from that woman's arm.

Shutov told the tale to Léa. What else could he offer her other than that country of his, rediscovered in books? During that very cold winter, two years before, at the start of their love affair, they would read Tolstoy almost every day. The attic was heated by a little cast-iron stove connected to the chimney hatch, the scent of tea mingled with that of the fire and the glow from the flames flickered across the pages of the book.

'You see, people are always saying: "Oh, Tolstoy. A ver-r-r-y R-r-russian novel. A mighty river, an impetuous, capricious torrent!" Not true! A mighty river, agreed, but under control, thanks to the lock gates of well-proportioned chapters. Indeed, a rather French structure, you might say.'

Shutov now attempts a mocking sneer but drunkenness has turned his face into a mask too weary for such contortions. Besides, that image of the lock gates isn't bad. And the memory of those evenings reading in front of the fire is still so tender, so raw.

He would also quote Chekhov: 'In a short story, cut the beginning and the end. That's where most of the lies are told.' Léa listened with daunting eagerness. 'Playboys take women out for drives in open-top cars,' Shutov thought with a smile. 'Destitute writers treat them to the Russian classics.' On a boat just about to leave a Crimea put to the torch by the Revolution, the young Nabokov was playing chess. The game was moving in an unusual and enthralling direction and when he finally tore himself away from the chequered board, the land of his birth had already vanished from sight! An empty expanse of sea, the cry of a gull, no regrets. For the time being . . .

'I got carried away like an idiot when I told her about that missed leave-taking . . .' Shutov remembers. The aesthete, Nabokov, cared more about an elegant metaphor than the land of his fathers. And *Lolita* was his punishment. A nauseating book, one that flatters the worst instincts of the Western bourgeoisie . . .

This verdict, he recalls, provoked one of those sparring matches in which Léa used to come to the defence of writers assailed by Shutov.

'But hold on, listen to this sentence,' she exclaimed

that evening. 'Nabokov writes: "His diction was as blurred as a moist lump of sugar." It's absolutely brilliant! You can feel it in your mouth. You can picture the man talking like that. You must admit it's very powerful!'

'Herculean! As I sit here, I can just picture our pretty Vladimir sucking his sugar lump. But it's not "brilliant", Léa. It's clever, there's a difference. And furthermore your Nabo couldn't care less whose accent this is. If it were a prisoner being tortured it wouldn't make any difference. He writes like a butterfly collector: he catches a beautiful insect, kills it with formalin, impales it on a pin. And he does the same thing with words . . .'

Shutov went on reviling Nabokov but Léa's eyes glazed over; she seemed to be observing a scene enacted beyond the walls of the dovecote, far from their conversation. 'She can see a man playing chess on the deck of a ship and his native shore sinking below the horizon.' Shutov fell silent, listened to the hiss of the rain on the roof.

The next day, somewhat embarrassed, Léa had informed him that she must 'pay a duty visit' to her mother. They set off together. This trip would mean more to Shutov than the year he had spent in New York, more than all his wanderings across Europe, more, even, than his time in Afghanistan on military service.

And yet it was just three days spent in an unpicturesque region to the north of the Ardennes. Cold, fog, hills

22

covered in shivering woodland. And to crown the lack of tourist appeal, a faded hoarding in the middle of a patch of wasteland announcing the imminent opening of a 'leisure centre'.

He found himself back in a period he had never known, not being French, and fell a little in love with it. The designs on the paper lining the wardrobe in his hotel room were like those seen on the walls of houses under demolition. Before the mirror Shutov experienced vertigo: all those faces from bygone days superimposed on one another in the greenish reflection! He ran his hand over the top of the wardrobe (a place that harbours treasures abandoned by travellers). On this occasion the treasure was an ancient copy of the local newspaper, dated 16 May 1981 . . .

Shutov read it while Léa had supper with her mother. He had been given leave not to show himself, to avoid introductions. 'You see, the difference in our ages practically makes me a paedophile. On the other hand, if you insist, I could propose to your mother . . .' Léa had laughed, relieved. 'That would kill me . . .'

They spent those three days going for walks, nestled close together under a big umbrella. Léa showed him her school, the little station (closed years ago) and, in a loop in the river Sormonne, a little wood where in her teens she used to come to write her first poems, believing that this activity called for an appropriately bucolic setting. Now, amid the winter squalls, the river was bleak, hostile. 'Bizarrely,' thought Shutov, 'this grey atmosphere is conducive to poetry,' and he saw an echo of the same conclusion reflected in Léa's eyes.

On one of those evenings, wandering the streets alone, he walked into the Café de la Gare, opposite the disused station. The customers seemed to know one another so well that for a stranger their conversational exchanges, in fragments of allusive sentences, remained Delphic. An old man seated at the table next to him began speaking in a tone that, while not directly addressed to the intruder, implied a welcome. Shutov turned to him and, almost without his being aware of it, a conversation was struck up: the streets of the little town became peopled with characters at once humble and heroic. The hills awoke beneath the clash of arms, were covered in soldiers. Close to the bridge ('it was narrower in those days, they altered it after the war') infantrymen, their faces grimy with dust, were retreating, firing at the enemy. 'We didn't have much ammunition. We had to cut and run. The Fritzes had got very close. At least the ones spraying us had. Then it was night. We thought we could get to the forest. Well, we hoped we could . . . It was our machine-gunner, a fellow called Claude Baud, who saved us. He'd been hit in the leg but he went on firing. He was knelt there in a pool of blood . . .'

Customers would come in and greet the man, speaking very loudly: 'How's it going, Henri? On good form, as ever?' The youths playing table football would repeat: 'How's it going, Henri?' in mocking tones, whispering a rhyme, the sense of which was lost on Shutov. The man seemed to hear neither one lot nor the other. But he replied to Shutov's questions without asking him to speak up. He even recognized his foreign accent, that 'r', an incorrigible giveaway . . . Léa came in, called out:

24

'Hello, Henri. All right then?' and signalled to Shutov for them to go.

That night in his hotel room he thought again about the old man at the Café de la Gare. An ill-lit room, a window looking out over rusty tracks, words from a past that interests no one. He felt very close to this man, to the dreary houses in the little town and the hillsides plunged in frosty darkness. 'I could live here. Yes, I could feel at home in this part of the world . . .' Confusedly, Léa must have sensed that for Shutov this trip would be a journey back to his true self.

The moonlight has moved away from the top-floor flat in the building across the street. The moon hangs above the rooftops and blue brilliance floods the attic. Enough to read the titles of the books Léa has stacked up ready for her move. Titles that chart the chronology of his love for her. Their readings, their quarrels on the subject of a particular author . . . Then comes a swift demolition job, it all falls down, crash! He knocks over one of the piles, the volumes scatter on the floor. Which book were they talking about the day the first crack appeared? Maybe it was this collection of short stories. In one of them a woman was reunited with the man she had once loved and together they sped down a snowy slope on a toboggan . . . Ah, so during that trip to the Ardennes, he had seen himself as a Chekhovian lover. I love you, Nadenka . . .

Three o'clock in the morning, the day has arrived when Léa will come to collect her cardboard boxes, the remnants of her life in Shutov's life. After she has left he will go on talking to himself, a little like the old man at the Café de la Gare.

He realizes he has never said anything to Léa that was vitally important. Has not dared, has not known how to. He has wasted so many days (miraculous days, days made for love) proclaiming the poet's sacred mission, railing against the intellectual establishment. At first she used to listen to him with the reverence prophets enjoy. Literary Paris fascinated her and Shutov seemed like a very well-established writer. The illusion lasted less than a year. The time it took for a young woman from the provinces to get her bearings and realize that this man was, in fact, no more than a marginal figure. And even his past as a dissident, which in the old days had given Shutov a certain aura, was becoming a flaw, or at least a sign of how prehistoric he was: just think, a dissident from the eighties of the previous century, an opposition figure exiled from a country that had since been erased from all the maps! 'The early eighties, the time when I was a baby,' Léa must have told herself. Now her affection became tinged

26

with pity. She sought to extricate Shutov from his isolation. And this was the start of a war neither could win.

'We're not in the nineteenth century now!' she would argue. 'Books are a product like any other . . . Well, because they're for sale, of course! All right, go ahead. Do what Bulgakov did. Write to be published thirty years from now. After you're dead.'

Shutov would grow heated, give examples of writers who had been rediscovered: Nietzsche, and those forty copies of *Thus Spake Zarathustra,* published at the author's expense and given to his friends.

'Fine. Give me your manuscript and in an hour I'll come back with forty copies. You can sign the first one for your Australian neighbour, and he'll wedge open his skylight with it. You've got the wrong period, Ivan! These days the most popular man in France is a footballer, not a poet . . .'

'In some countries that period survives!'

'Really? In Outer Manchuria, I suppose.'

'No. In Russia . . .'

These duels had an indirect consequence: Shutov began to dream of the Russia he had not seen for twenty years and where, he believed, a life persisted, rocked to sleep by well-loved lines of verse. A park beneath golden foliage, a woman walking in silence, like the heroine of a poem.

That image of a skylight wedged open with a manuscript was a milestone. He sensed a certain arrogance in Léa, that pert humour, known as *gouaille,* so relished by the French (he had never understood why). She began

27

spending time away often, on the pretext of her journalism classes or doing work experience at a publisher's.

One day he had to go out early and downstairs on the lid of a dustbin he noticed a large black leather bag. In the metro a doubt assailed him: that bundle had not been a bag. Passing again at noon he did not see it but guessed it had been Léa's old jacket. A frayed lining, leather curves moulded to the shape of her body . . . The intense sadness that overcame him surprised him. Now, at last, he felt capable of putting into words the fleeting images that were the only truth in his life: that old jacket, Léa's arm flung out across the covers in her sleep . . . She came back in the evening clutching a parcel to her chest. Shutov's latest manuscript. Returned by a publisher. They ate supper in silence, then very quickly he flew into a rage against the 'pygmyism', as he called it, of the current literary world. Léa must have taken pity on him because she murmured in a less brittle voice, yes, her old voice: 'Don't be silly, Ivan. You're not a failure at all. You're like a . . . Yes, an explosion still waiting to be heard.'

From that evening onwards she became even more remote.

But amid this waning of their love affair, an impressive recovery occurred. Shutov was invited onto a television programme! Bizarrely, for a novel he had published three years previously, which had enjoyed no success. The publicist resolved the mystery: 'You talked about Afghanistan in it: and now, with everything that's happening there . . .' It was the book in which a young soldier burst into tears at the sight of an old woman and her dog killed in an artillery bombardment.

In telling Léa about the invitation Shutov chose to feign indifference and even made one or two mocking remarks ('Just you wait. I'll torpedo their ratings . . .'). But in reality he felt as if he were making his last throw. In this young woman's eyes he could once again become the writer who initiated her knowledgeably into the secrets of the profession.

He bought a plain blue shirt, because 'stripes cause strobing on the screen,' he explained. Léa went with him, made up as if she were taking part in the broadcast herself.

This was due to go out around midnight. 'After the gameshows, the football and the rest. That's their scale of values.' Shutov quickly resolved not to allow himself any rancour. On television one must smile, be a little simplistic, no nuances. 'Break a leg,' whispered Léa and, tense as he was, Shutov gave a start before remembering this strange custom. From that moment onwards it all felt quite surreal to him.

Dreamlike, too, was the late-night scheduling, which made the participants seem like conspirators (or spirits) gathered, ironically, around a garishly lit table. But above all, this obligation to be a smiling idiot. Nobody demanded it, yet a mysterious force clamped these foolish grins onto their faces, made them ogle like prostitutes soliciting custom.

Perched on a high stool ('just like the ones in a tarts' bar,' thought Shutov), he studied the 'panel'. There was a young black francophone writer, with a grin like an Uncle Ben advertisement. A Chinese man, with a sly air, his gaze shifty behind his thin glasses. And, for good measure, himself, Shutov, a Russian. Three living proofs of the globalization of French literature. Just across from Shutov the make-up girl was giving the finishing touches to the face of a . . . What could one call him? Journalist, writer, editor, member of several prize juries, a well-known mediacrat whom Shutov used to refer to as 'one of the literary Mafia', and at whom he must now smile. On this man's left they had just seated a psychologist who specialized in happiness, a state of mind rare in rich countries. The psychologist was talking to his neighbour, a young woman dressed like a Halloween witch. Finally a latecomer appeared, a woman in her fifties with greying hair and a handsome, faded face. Blinded by the lights, she wandered this way and that around the table until an assistant showed her to her seat, next to Shutov. He met her gaze, the intelligence of which was at odds with the smooth pink of her make-up. She was the only one not smiling.

The broadcast began. The African was on first and revealed himself to be a brilliant professional. Everything about his little performance was polished: his voice, his laughter, his lilting delivery; then a veritable comic interlude in which, quoting from his novel, he played the parts of both the rich lover and the cunning mistress, amid a whole host of relatives, storytellers and tribal magicians. A born actor.

After such a display the Chinese writer, despite his obsequious facial expressions, appeared dull. This was because he could hardly speak French. And yet this was the language he purported to write in and in which he was published by one of the best houses in Paris . . . What Shutov heard sounded, yet again, like something from a surrealist play. 'Yang is joined to yin . . . so yang with yin is making . . . And Confucius is saying . . . Red dragon mountain . . . Yin completes yang . . .' These last words were repeated so many times that the presenter himself became confused: 'So your character, yin fact – excuse me – in fact . . .'

But Shutov's performance was a real disaster. He began with a long, elegant sentence: the duty incumbent on a writer to bear witness, the quest for truth, the way the psychology of the characters can subvert the author's own preconceptions. For example, a battle-hardened soldier, confronted by the bodies of an old woman and her dog, bursting into tears. The presenter scented danger in this monologue and, as a good chairman, found a way to limit the damage: 'So, according to your book, it seems as if the Russians have a lot to answer for . . .' This journalistic vagueness created an opening for a recovery. But Shutov was already getting out of his depth. His tirade was compressed like a concertina, in it the writer's mission, the Taliban, Tolstoy rereading Stendhal to write the Battle of the Borodino, surface-to-air rockets, and the obscenity of aestheticism in a book about the war were all mixed up together . . . A gleam of compassion appeared in the presenter's eyes. 'So there we have it,' he summed up. 'Can it ever be possible to write about war in a novel?' This coup de grâce saved Shutov. He froze, his cheeks burning with shame, and with only one thought in his head: 'Léa was watching all that.'

The contributions of the others gradually distanced him from the appalled dummy he had turned into. 'When a man caresses his sexual partner,' the psychologist of happiness was saying, 'the nucleus of her dorso-median thalamus begins to . . .' The young witch novelist took up the tale, her eyes widening in a trance: 'The other is always the bringer of evil . . . The evil we refuse to acknowledge in ourselves . . .' It was already past midnight and the dreamlike aura was rapidly intensifying. Shutov felt less ridiculous. The tension within him finally relaxed, giving way to a melancholy clarity.

He told himself that this mildly weird charade was being played out in a country that had given the world Promethean geniuses, whose words had once confronted exile, death and, worse still, attacks by philistines. A prophetic daring, lives sacrificed on the altar of truth . . . In his youth that was how he had seen this great and ancient literature. Now, on the other side of the table, there was this elegantly smiling Chinese writer, whose books had been rewritten by an obscure editor (a living author brought to life by a ghost). On his left was this young woman setting out to shock the viewers with her demonic appearance. Facing him, an African from a land covered in millions of corpses was spinning pornographic yarns, lubricious anecdotes laced with folklore of dubious authenticity . . .

Shutov did not grasp what it was that dispelled this feeling of absurdity. His neighbour, the woman with greying hair, had a faint voice, or, rather, she employed

32

no vocal tricks. It seemed as if she had serenely come to terms with the rules of this stupid game: on television, speaking last at midnight, a woman with her looks has no chance. Pensively, her head bowed, she met no one's eyes. It seemed to Shutov as if she were addressing him alone.

The story is very simple, she was saying, a woman loves a very young man who is hooked on drugs. After a year and a half of struggle she manages to save him. A month later he meets a girl of his own age and leaves.

'In fact, the book starts when it's all over for my heroine. I think that's how it is in our lives. When you expect nothing more, life opens up to what is really important . . .'

Suddenly, still in her calm voice, she addressed Shutov: 'Just now you were quoting Chekhov . . . Yes, he encouraged us to cut the opening and the ending of a story. But I don't know if Doctor Chekhov's remedy can cure a novel. In any event my heroine comes to life in the part of the story he advised us to cut.'

And without any change of tone, without declaiming, she read several sentences from the book open in front of her. A forest in winter, a woman on a footpath with a brown carpet of fallen leaves, a soothing, acrid scent, grief turning to joy at each step taken down a misty avenue of trees . . .

The broadcast ended. Shutov remained seated, his eyes half closed. A forest in the mist, a figure disappearing at the end of a pathway . . . A technician roused him to retrieve his microphone. In the corridor, near the make-up room, he caught up with the grey-haired

33

woman. 'Why did you take part in that farce?' He did
not have the courage to ask her this, murmuring instead:
'I was grateful for Chekhov! Thanks to you I didn't
look so stupid. But I didn't catch the name of your
book . . .'

'*After Her Life*. I'll send it to you. I read yours when
it came out. I've read all your books. But I didn't expect
to see you here. Why did you come?'

They smiled, imagining the excuses writers generally
concoct: my publisher was very insistent, I was there
to hold the line against dumbing down . . . And at that
moment he saw Léa.

'That was fantastic!' she declared, kissing him on the
cheek. He turned to introduce her to the grey-haired
woman but the latter had already gone into the make-
up room. 'No, it was great,' Léa went on. 'It made you
want to read the books. Especially that Chinese writer.
I really liked him. What he said about the yin and the
yang was really deep. But I thought the woman next
to you, the one who came on last, was, like, hopeless.
Did you see how she was made up? She looked . . .'

The 'hopeless' woman emerged from the make-up
room and Shutov saw her moving away. As she walked
along she was rubbing her face with a tissue and from
a distance one might have thought she was wiping away
tears.

In the taxi Léa's enthusiasm knew no bounds. Shutov
reflected that the stupid media magic had given him a
makeover and perhaps what had felt like a wretched
failure would give their partnership a new lease of life.
Léa praised the young witch's performance. She thought

34

it clever how she had 'only just got away with it'. Then she went back to the woman reading a few lines from her book. 'I simply can't make that one out. It was a real clanger putting her on. She's, like, old and dreary, you know, not sexy at all. And she looked as if she was bored out of her skull. It was lucky for her you mentioned Chekhov. It gave her the chance to show off a bit . . .'

Shutov touched Léa's hand and murmured very calmly: 'You don't need to go on, Léa. I know you're not as moronic as you make out.'

Then he quickly regretted this undiplomatic remark, knowing that people never forgive you for refusing to join in games of self-deception.

Nor was Shutov deceived by Léa's 'infidelities'. The word had a farcical ring to it – he found others ('she sleeps with a friend from time to time'), preferring to act like a writer: to live at arm's length from the situation so as not to suffer from it and one day to be able to describe it. But the posture of the detached observer is a delusion. He suffered, despised his own suffering, lapsed into mocking cynicism, re-emerged to clear his beloved of all suspicion, behaved, in fact, precisely like the hero of one of those psychological novels whose authors meticulously flaunt their knowledge of the human psyche, just the type of book he detested.

What he succeeded best at was turning a blind eye. He had already noticed that, with increasing age, this exercise became easier.

That evening, too, he would have forced himself to see nothing, had Léa not decided to present him with an illusion of love regained.

It was a bleak dusk in early February, reflected in the tarmac was a whole subterranean world into which you could have hurled yourself and disappeared. Shutov was on his way back from a meeting (a publisher had been explaining to him just why the subject of his novel was unsaleable). Unable to brave the crowd in the metro, he had climbed all the way up to Ménilmontant on foot. Just a little more pain might make his life unbearable and what then? Cut his own throat? String himself up? Such things are fine in a novel, but in real life the final straw took the form of an overturned dustbin below their block of flats, a cornucopia spilling out its household rubbish. Not something to slit your carotid artery over, my good scribblers!

As he mounted the narrow spiral staircase he could already smell the aroma of a wood fire. Behind the door of the dovecote there was a ripple of silky music but in the time it took to locate the keyhole Shutov experienced conflicting sensations: within his attic a party was in full swing yet he, a man clad in a rain-soaked overcoat, no longer possessed the right key to enter into this convivial life.

Léa had prepared a dinner, lit the fire and candles, the illusion was complete. Right down to the simulation of their readings in the old days. At the end of the meal she declared in somewhat exaggerated tones: 'I've just been reading Chekhov's "Vanka". You know, it's heartbreaking. I wept . . . No, I really cried my eyes out!'

Shutov studied her. An attractive young woman smoking nonchalantly, curled up in a feline pose ('a hackneyed image,' he quibbled). And two years earlier, that girl rather strapped for cash in a telephone booth

37

at the Gare de l'Est. A striking but natural change: the swift adaptability of youth, the vigour of a life taking wing. Journalism classes which, in France, lead to everything, a group of friends her own age. And this still useful, ageing man, whom it would be easy to get rid of. A man she feels like cheering up, one winter's evening, by lighting up his garret with a scattering of sparks from her youthful, free, intense existence . . .

'You know, Léa, I've never been crazy about Chekhov.'

In Shutov's voice there was the hint of an over-taut string, despite the banality of his observation. Drowsy as she was, she must have noticed it.

'I see. I thought you . . . Look, remember you used to swear by him! His sentences like lancet stabs. You were the one who used to say that . . .'

His elbows on the table, he massaged his brow then looked at Léa and realized that what she saw was this face creased by a whole evening of pulling forced expressions.

'No, I'm not talking about his style,' he replied. 'He's a storyteller without equal. Concision, the art of detail, humour. It's all there. I bow to him! What goes against the grain is all that compassion of Chekhov's. Granted, he's a humanist. He takes pity on an aristocrat who's blown all her money in Paris and returns to Russia to bemoan her lot in her beloved cherry orchard. He feels sorry for three provincial women who can't manage to leave their own backyard and go to Moscow. He laments the fate of a whole crowd of doctors, petty gentry, eternal students and—'

'But hold on, those were people who suffered! He shows how society broke their dreams, how the mediocrity of their period suffocated them . . .'

'That's true . . . But you see, Léa, Chekhov died in 1904 and very shortly after that, some fifteen, twenty years later, in fact, in the very same country where his heroes had spent their time cursing their woes in the shade of cherry orchards in bloom . . . In that same country, millions of human beings were brutally exterminated, without any humanist worrying about their "broken dreams", as you call them.'

'Sorry, Ivan. You've lost me there. You're surely not going to blame Chekhov for everyone who died in the Gulag?'

'Why not? Well, no. Certainly not! Only, after what's happened in my country, I think I have the right to say this to Chekhov: by all means weep, dear Master, for your petty noblemen, refined and sensitive as they are, but leave us to weep for our millions of wretched yokels!'

He fell silent, then mumbled in conciliatory tones: 'I should have put that a bit differently . . .'

The Chekhov story, 'Vanka', that had entranced Léa was one of Shutov's favourites. But to talk about it over this dinner, which was a replica of their evenings in the old days . . . No! Léa had been using young Vanka as a backdrop for her masquerade of affection. 'Perhaps this is how she wants to take her leave of me. An amicable divorce in an elegiac setting, to avoid a brutal breach. In fact, she set me a trap and I walked straight into it. Poor old writer! What

39

a hopeless expert in the human psyche! An ill-shod shoemaker, indeed . . .'

'Look Ivan, you've got it all wrong. That story's not about a petty nobleman at all. It's about a little peasant boy sent away to be an apprentice in the city and his master maltreats him. All he's got is his grandfather. He writes to him. Not knowing the address, he writes on the envelope: "To my grandfather, Konstantin Makarych. The country." He posts the letter and waits for the reply. That scene knocked me out! What shocks me is your lack of sensitivity. You're Russian but that story is totally lost on you . . .'

'I'm not Russian, Léa. I'm Soviet. So you see I'm filthy, stupid and vicious. Very different from all those Michel Strogoffs and Prince Myshkins the French are crazy about. Sorry . . .'

She stared at him with a stubborn, hostile air, her tone of voice refusing to acknowledge Shutov's rueful smile.

'That's just it. Your generation of Russians were so programmed by the totalitarian regime that it's no longer possible to communicate with you. Even on a mundane level, I mean. You've never learned the slightest tolerance. Everything's all black or all white. In the end it gets tiring. I do my head in trying to make you see . . .'

Léa went on with her speech for the prosecution and he sensed that any minute now the verdict would be delivered: she would tell him she was leaving. She would not even need to argue her case, he had just made himself a sitting target . . . The attic without her? 'Just a little more pain might make my life unbearable . . .'

He ran through all the routes for retreat in his mind: apologize, laugh, feign contrition, admit to being genetically modified by communism . . . Meanwhile she was saying: 'As long as you cling to your past in Soviet slavery . . .' (In a brief moment of distraction Shutov glanced at Léa's arms: 'She'll never know how beautiful her arm can be.') ' . . . And if you don't feel free you crush other people. You don't respect anyone's inner feelings. I find Vanka writing to his grandfather really upsetting. But you couldn't give a damn. Well look, I think we need to have a serious talk, because quite honestly . . .'

He choked from the pressure of words held back and, to begin with, his voice was a whisper, broken, expressionless: 'Of course, Léa. We'll have a talk whenever you like. But before that I want to tell you a little story. Quite Chekhovian, by the way. I have it from a friend. He was an orphan. As a child he used to be sent with his comrades to gather vegetables on collective farms. On one occasion it was a kind of swede they had to dig up from more or less frozen soil. They were scrabbling about in the mud and suddenly my pal unearthed a skull, then a soldier's helmet. Their supervisor told him to go and take these to the farm management. He set off and spent a long time floundering across ploughed fields, then he stopped and . . . How can I put it? He realized that he was all alone on this earth. The low northern sky, icy fields as far as the eye could see, and himself with that skull and

41

the helmet in a bag. It's quite upsetting you know, for a child to confront such complete, almost cosmic, loneliness: himself, the sky, the mud under his feet and no one from whom he can expect a word of tenderness. No one in the whole universe! No grandfather to send a letter to . . . So, you see, I'm quits with Chekhov and his Vanka. As you'll have guessed, that little lad amid the fields was me.'

As it happened, his story would achieve nothing. It might even have furnished one more motive for their break-up: a refusal to share the past of someone you no longer love.

A wounded man can do no other, Shutov had learned this in the army. When hit, a body struggles against the first wave of pain, flails about, fights, then, overcome, goes rigid. During the final months of their relationship he had behaved like a wounded man embarking on his dance with death, resisting it, clutching it to his heart. Then one day in a crowded café he had gone rigid. 'In Russian, "*shut*" means "clown",' Léa was saying. 'A buffoon.' A sad clown, he had added, conscious that the word defined all too well what he had become.

A grey spring came, without savour: the emptiness of the streets at night, the blue of days that started for him at three o'clock in the afternoon and this attic, the only place where his life still had any kind of meaning. Thanks to those cardboard boxes Léa was going to take away.

And if anywhere else existed it was that park of thirty years ago in Leningrad, two shadowy figures walking slowly along beneath the autumn leaves, their breathing matched to the rhythm of a poem.

Drink helped him to believe that this country beneath the golden foliage still existed. This certainty became so intense that one day Shutov accomplished something which had earlier seemed inconceivable: he found an agency that obtained visas for Russia and now, once a fortnight, he packed a suitcase, booked a ticket. And did not go.

In the end he admired the dexterity with which Léa had transformed their relationship into a vague camaraderie. After two months' absence she began to show signs of life but now in the guise of an old friend, well disposed, devoid of passion. Asexual. It was in this guise that she telephoned him towards the middle of May. Her voice created a distance such that Shutov thought he must be speaking to a woman he had met during another period of his life. At the end of the conversation the old Léa gave herself away, but advisedly: 'Do you remember that coffee table I bought which is at your place? And my corner bookshelf? I'm going to come over with a friend who's got a car. But I wanted to let you know in advance . . . In fact, I've told him we were just good friends and I'd left those bits of furniture at your place for the time being. He doesn't need to come up if you'd prefer him not to . . .'

Shutov protested vehemently, afraid of seeming like a jealous old fogey. And in this way he got to see Léa's friend (the figure of a tall adolescent, a fine, harmonious face). He greeted him and retreated to the kitchen, heard them talking about their flat. They were discussing where they would put the pieces of furniture they were collecting. Involuntarily Shutov pictured himself in those rooms smelling of fresh paint, in their world . . . He was touched by the fervour they invested in their move. The young man carried the little set of shelves the way one carries a baby. And Shutov felt terribly old and disillusioned.

All that was left in his attic now was a few cardboard boxes, a bag of Léa's clothes and two piles of books. Occasionally Shutov would open a volume, leaf through it: people falling in and out of love, pain and pleasure, wisdom slowly gained and, at the end of the day, useless. Little psychological dissertations the French call 'novels'.

He could have written one of these slight works himself. Picturing Léa sometimes as a female Rastignac, sometimes as a fallen woman rescued by a wanderer with a heart of gold. What else could he invent? A little girl gone astray in the jungle of the capital, a cynical young woman on the make, a sleeping Madonna bathed in moonlight . . . A provincial woman corrupted by Paris, a Galatea awakened by her Pygmalion. All plausible but false.

There was more truth in that brief glimpse he had: wriggling through his skylight up to the waist, Shutov watched Léa and her friend crossing the courtyard, carrying the coffee table, and could see the rear of a car parked in the street. An evening in May, this young couple departing towards a luminous sequence of roads and journeys, towards that unpredictable abundance of tiny joys which is life. He felt a lump in his throat (how many times had he mocked authors who used that expression) and could have given all he possessed for this new-found love to be a happy one! The young people set the table down on the pavement, the boy opened the boot. And that was when Léa looked up and her gaze, hesitant at first, focused on the attic and the skylight . . . Shutov hid rapidly and remained bent double for a moment, panting as if he had been running, ashamed of having gained entry into a life where he no longer existed.

From now on a bitter contentment inhabited him: the relief of no longer desiring anything, of having so few objects around him, of experiencing no jealousy. Of no longer having to fight.

He could have lived in this peace of renunciation for a long time. But a week later Léa telephoned him and asked if she could come round the following day to complete the move. 'It really will be the very last time!' she said, reassuringly.

The very last time . . . 'Dying,' he thought, 'begins with ambiguous little phrases like this, well before any physical extinction.' He went over to the corner where Léa's things were stacked, crouched down, stroked the silk of a blouse. And sensed deep within himself someone who still wanted to desire, to love . . . 'Not to be taken for an old piece of furniture!' this other one cried out. To be able to kiss a woman's arm as she slept.

But above all, after that telephone call he realized he would not have the strength to be present at his own funeral in an attic that was about to be emptied of everything that was his life.

These are names more mysterious than hieroglyphs on a papyrus eroded by millennia. Out-of-date addresses, curiously brief telephone numbers. A whole lapsed world Shutov is trying to bring back to life as he leafs impatiently through the pages of a notebook retrieved from the depths of an old travelling bag. The bag he had with him when he left Russia twenty years ago . . . A papyrus, yes, the comparison is no exaggeration: since then a country has disappeared, cities have changed their names and the faces conjured up by the addresses survive only in Shutov's memory.

He glances at the window which is starting to turn pale. He has made his decision. At ten o'clock in the morning Léa will come with her friend and they will find no one here. The visa in his passport is still valid. He will go at once, as soon as he has found her address, the one who . . . A silhouette outlined by the autumn sun against the golden leaves.

She was called Yana. At the end of her studies she left Leningrad to go and work beyond the Urals. This he knows. Nothing more. The addresses in this notebook, like an encoded message, may perhaps lead him to this woman: a sequence of friends, who, stage by stage, may indicate the places where she made her home during that abyss of years.

One of them lives in western Siberia. Shutov telephones him, apologizes for calling him practically in the middle of the night, then realizes that over there, beyond the Urals, the sun is already at its zenith. What amazes him more is that the friend in question should be so little amazed. 'I see, so you're calling from Paris. I was there with my wife in April . . . Who? Yana? I think she taught at Tomsk University . . .' Shutov works through other numbers, talks to strangers, passes through three, five, ten time zones . . . But it is the surprise of that first conversation that remains the greatest: a man of his own age in a town in Siberia, responding as if there were nothing unusual in this, life goes on, and a couple of months earlier this former fellow student could have run into him in Paris.

Several sheets of paper lie before him, blackened with figures. He reaches the Far East and in Vladivostok a child's voice calls a grandmother to the telephone, a student at Leningrad University in the same year as Shutov, thirty years ago. 'So I'm old enough to be a grandfather,' he says to himself, conscious that his own exile had banished him from the chronology of human beings. His friends were living their lives, marrying, surrounding themselves with children and grandchildren, while he was transforming himself into an ageless ghost.

'Listen, Shutov, I know she went back to Leningrad, well, St Petersburg. She'd married a fellow who was in oil. Yes, you get the picture. And it didn't work out . . .

48

No, not the oil. The marriage. Wait, I've got her best friend's number. She'll be able to help you . . .'

Five minutes later Shutov is writing down the number of Yana's mobile telephone. Digits that magically encompass the shade of a remote feminine presence, days filled with autumn gold, declarations never hazarded.

It is half past eight in Paris, half past ten in St Petersburg. Shutov dials the number, but just before it rings he hangs up, goes into the bathroom, thrusts his face beneath the cold tap, splashes himself, drinks, clears his throat. Then smoothes down his wet hair in front of a mirror. He feels the hallucinatory clarity descending upon him that comes from a sleepless night, extreme tension, drink overcome. The sensation of being about to hurl himself into a void, like in the old days when bailing out of the cabin of an aircraft, but without the parachute's reassuring weight.

He dials again. In St Petersburg a mobile phone comes to life. A male voice, strangely rhythmical at first: 'The Prime Minister's Boeing has just landed. Southern districts of the city will experience extreme traffic disruption . . .' A woman's voice, closer: 'Yes. It's to your left just beyond the bridge, but steer clear of the Nevsky . . .' After a moment Shutov realizes that the male voice is that of a newscaster and that the woman's voice is speaking to the driver of a car.

'Hello, what? Oh, Ivan! I was thinking about you only the other day, and do you know why? Hold on, I'm just going to park . . .'

This interruption allows Shutov to gather his wits, to make a landing, he thinks. His feet touch the ground, the parachute drags him along, then the canopy collapses, deflates on the grass and now at last certainty imposes itself: safe and sound.

'Yes, my son came across your name on a website for French books. He does publicity for a publishing house. He was surprised to see a Russian name. I told him we used to know one another . . .'

The banality of these words is disconcerting. Even wounding. Shutov feels it like a pinprick: nothing serious and yet it jars. He interrupts the person who has not yet become Yana: 'You see, I'm coming to Lenin . . . St Petersburg, today.'

'Oh, what a shame!'

The disappointment is sincere.

'How do you mean? Don't you want us to meet?' Shutov's tone is almost aggressive.

'But of course I do! It's a shame because you've missed half the celebrations . . . Wait. Where have you been? The whole world's been talking of nothing else. Blair's plane has just landed. It's the tercentenary of the city . . . A hotel? That'll be difficult. But we'll sort something out, I work in the hotel business. Or if not . . . Right, we'll see when you're here. I've got to go now, Ivan. I'm late already. Make a careful note of my new address . . .'

Shutov's departure is a rush to escape. Any minute now Léa and her friend will be knocking at the door. He throws whatever comes to hand into his old travelling bag. Writes a note, rings his Australian neighbour's bell, gives him the key, runs to catch a taxi. And at the airport, as on the telephone, speaks his mother

50

tongue for the first time in many long years. The Russian airline representative reassures him: the flight will be half empty, the stampede took place yesterday, everyone wanted to get there for the opening of the festivities.

In the air Shutov hovers between sleep and unreality. He is on his way to see a woman of whom all he can remember, thirty years on, is a luminous silence, the clear outline of a face. Quite a different woman is now driving beside the Neva in her car. And thinking of him? She works in a hotel (he pictures an establishment from the Soviet era, a matron ensconced at the reception desk), she has a son, a 'publicist' (how do you say that in Russian?), but above all, she does not seem to be terrified by the interstellar chasm that has come between them. Does she recall their encounters in those parks where the sunsets would come and fade away over the Baltic?

In mid-flight he falls asleep, carrying into his dreams the question that causes so much pain: 'But if I were not coming, would the lives of the people I've been telephoning continue just as before? And Yana's life? So why come?'

II

II

In his mind Shutov has contrived to add thirty years to the face of the girl he had known. To age her with a silvery patina, a fine web of wrinkles . . . The woman who opens the door to him has certainly grown older, but differently. He pictured a physical consolidation, a heaviness which, when he was young, women acquired from a certain age, their lives being hardly conducive to refinement. A woman worker at the controls of a steamroller was not such a rare occurrence in the old days . . . Yana kisses him with a twittering welcome and, making a rapid visual adjustment, he has to accept this slim woman with ochreish blonde hair and a youthful appearance.

'She looks like . . . Léa!' The realization is so disconcerting that now nothing else surprises him. Not the length of the corridor, nor all these rooms leading into one another (a communal flat?), nor even this invitation of Yana's: 'Come along, I'm going to show you the jacuzzi . . .' They arrive in an extremely spacious bathroom, half of which is occupied by an oval bath. Two plumbers are busily engaged around this pink monster. 'Hey! Watch out for the gold plating!' Yana calls out, at once severe and teasing. The men respond with grunts of reassurance. She winks at Shutov and leads him into a large empty room.

55

'Look! This'll be the drawing room. Leave your luggage, I'll give you a guided tour.'

They resume their stroll through this very white interior, lit by clusters of halogen spotlights, which Shutov hesitates to call a 'flat'. As he put his bag down he had experienced a childish fear: would he be able to find it again in this labyrinth? Yana walks on, smiling, explaining. The kitchen, the dining room, another dining room, 'in case we ever have a full house', a bathroom but with an ordinary bath, a bedroom, another bedroom . . . She says 'we' and Shutov does not dare to ask if she is married . . . He remembers that she works in the hotel business. So could this perhaps be a suite for letting? He lacks the Russian words to translate such a new reality.

He had noticed this deficiency a short while earlier. The taxi dropped him at the edge of a district closed to traffic. He was walking along, light, curious, relaxed – a demeanour appropriate, he thought, for his status as a foreigner, whose clothes and movements would not pass unremarked. Very quickly he realized that no one was paying him any attention. The people were dressed as they would be in a city in the West, perhaps a little less casually. And if he did stand out in the midst of this summery throng it was thanks to his own clothes looking tired. Disconcerted, Shutov had told himself he was not far off being taken for a tramp . . .

'And here, you see, this part of the ceiling will open up. We'll be able to see the sky. We need to take advantage of every ray of sunlight. We're not in Florida . . .'

56

Shutov subjects Yana to the intense scrutiny an explorer would reserve for a new species awaiting classification. She is reminiscent of Léa . . . No, this is a false similarity. Quite simply she corresponds to a certain type of European woman: svelte, sleekly blonde, face carefully smoothed of wrinkles.

'So will your family live here?' He would have liked to talk to Yana about their past but he must first ask conventional questions like this.

'As a matter of fact, the move was planned for tomorrow. But with these celebrations we had to put everything off . . . As a result, if you'd like to sleep here . . . Finding a good hotel won't be easy. We've got four in our chain but with the number of VIPs arriving, you'd feel as if you were in a fortress under siege, there are ten bodyguards at every entrance. So, welcome to my humble abode! Two of the rooms are already more or less furnished . . . And this is another corridor, you see. When we joined all the flats together we fixed up a two-room suite for my son. Vlad, may we come in?'

The young man who welcomes them looks strangely familiar: a gangling youth in T-shirt and jeans, a fair-haired twenty-year-old such as one might come across in London, or Amsterdam, or an American sitcom.

'Whisky? Martini? Beer?' Vlad offers with a smile, indicating a tray with an array of bottles. 'So this is it,' thinks Shutov. 'We've reached the stage of irony.' At first Russia copied these Western fashions, now they delight in pastiching them. Near the window is a coat rack surmounted by a plaster cast of Andy Warhol's shaggy head. Across from that a scarlet banner, with letters in gold: 'Forward to the Victory of Communist Toil!' A poster of Madonna, with Second World War medals attached to her chest. A television set with a screen at least three feet wide: a car comes to a halt on a mountain top, facing a magical sunrise. 'To be on time, when every second counts!' says the warm, virile voice of the commercial . . .

Vlad sits down at his computer. Yana smoothes a tuft of his hair. Annoyed, he moves away: 'Hey, stop that, Ma . . .' A momentary look crosses the mother's face, which Shutov recognizes with a sudden intake of breath.

'I've checked,' says Vlad. 'They don't market you too well in Europe.' Shutov bends over and is stunned to recognize his photograph.

'I'm not too well . . . known. Besides . . . I didn't know my books were listed on the Internet. In fact, I don't have a computer. I write everything by hand, then I type it out . . .'

Vlad and Yana laugh uncertainly: their guest has a somewhat ponderous sense of humour.

There is a muffled cough in the room next door, which relieves the situation. Through the half-open door Shutov catches sight of patterned wallpaper, the foot of a bed covered in a dark green blanket, like those provided on night trains in the old days . . .

'Yes, this is pure Ionesco!' Yana exclaims, anticipating his question. 'No, I must tell you. We managed to clear four communal flats and that was on two floors. Eleven rooms to be joined up, twenty-six people to be relocated! A property-management manoeuvre crazier than a game of chess. We've rehoused them all. For some of them we had to make a triple swap. Piles of paper, lots of red tape, backhanders. I'll spare you the details. In the end both floors were ours. There was just this room. With a house-warming gift in it! Yes, this old man (he's paraplegic, poor thing), who was due to be admitted to an old people's home ten days ago. And then, what happens? We have this wretched tercentenary, the city's all closed off. And lo and behold, we have to live with a grandfather who doesn't even belong to us! Well, actually, the day after tomorrow he's going to be moved. But, as I say, it's like the play by Ionesco, you remember, that flat where there's a corpse and no one knows how to get rid of it . . .'

The comparison is rather dubious and to retrieve the situation, Yana knocks on the door. 'Georgy Lvovich, may we come in to say hello?' To Shutov she murmurs: 'I think he's a bit deaf. And what's more, he's lost . . . the power of speech.'

It is a slip of the tongue, this 'power of speech'; she should have said: 'he's dumb' or 'he has aphasia'. But they are already entering the room.

An old man lies on a bed constructed from nickel-plated tubes, of a type Shutov believed had long since disappeared. On his night table is a cup in which a teabag is macerating, and the glint of thick bifocal glasses. His eyes return Shutov's look with perfect lucidity. 'It's all been arranged, Georgy Lvovich. You'll be in good hands very soon.' Yana speaks in loud and artificially cheerful tones. 'The doctors are going to take you right out into the country. You'll be able to hear the birds singing . . .' The old man's face remains unchanged, maintaining its air of grave detachment, with no hint of bitter tension, showing no inclination to make contact through facial expression in default of language. Does he understand everything? Almost certainly, even though his only response is to close his eyes. 'Fine. Have a good rest, Georgy Lvovich. Vlad's here all the time if you need anything . . .' With a little tilt of her head, Yana indicates to Shutov that the visit is at an end. As he backs out he notices a book lying on the bed: the old man's hand is touching the volume as if it were a living being.

Yana closes the door and raises her eyebrows with a sigh. 'For someone of his generation it would have been better to depart this world before the latest upheavals. Do you know what monthly pension he gets? One thousand two hundred. Roubles. Forty dollars. That's enough to strike you dumb. After fighting in the war all the way to Berlin. But you know, these days, nobody could give a damn! And it's a crying shame we can't hear his voice any more. He was a professional singer. His neighbours told me that in the war, well, during the siege of Leningrad, he went out with a whole choir to sing to the troops . . .'

She starts walking again, stops in front of an open window. A bright fresh May evening, strangely autumnal in feel. 'You see, when we were young we didn't have time to talk to people like him. But now he's the one who can't speak . . .'

Shutov is preparing to tell her why he came, to remind her of their youth . . . 'Guess what this is!' Yana insists,

60

resuming her tour guide's voice. A huge marble hand placed on an occasional table in the entrance hall to the apartment. 'It's Slava's hand!' Perceiving Shutov's puzzled expression, she pulls a surprised face, as if failing to recognize 'Slava's hand' were a flagrant breach of taste. 'Yes, Rostropovich's hand. He's a friend. It was my idea. Everyone has visiting cards these days and I thought our guests could leave their cards in this hand . . . People generally put out one of those earthenware things but a hand is much more original . . .' Shutov reflects that in the days of his youth he never saw anyone in Russia take out a visiting card. Yes, their youth . . .

'You know, I didn't come here for the celebration . . .' he says with slightly gruff insistence. 'I thought that . . .' Yana's mobile phone rings. 'Yes, I'm on my way. I was in a traffic jam. Well have you seen the chaos? I'll be there in a quarter of an hour . . .'

She shows Shutov the two bedrooms he may choose between and races away. That 'owner's tour' of hers was also, in fact, a way of taking evasive action. Yana kept on talking, laughing, addressing other people, as if she were afraid of what he might have to say about their past. But how, in any case, could he have brought up those distant days that still form a bond between them? 'I love you, Nadenka . . .' Shutov smiles. Yes, he could have quoted Chekhov.

He leaves the apartment five minutes after Yana. The gravitational pull of the city sucks him in, thrusts him towards a life in which he will be himself once again, speaking the language of his childhood, immersed in a human mass to which he belongs by origin. He feels like an old actor, who has been performing in an over-long play ('my life in the West,' he thinks), now casting aside his tattered finery and losing himself in the crowd.

Not far from the Admiralty policemen bar his way. He makes a detour and encounters another street closed. Heads towards the Palace Embankment and finds himself thrust back into Millionaya Street. He tries to argue, then, naively, demands an explanation, and finally walks away, no longer trying to reach the site of the celebrations. The festival is at its height, so close, just a few blocks away, yet inaccessible, as on a tortuous path in a nightmare. 'You should have read the papers,' grunts one of the policemen. 'They showed all the closed-off districts . . .'

He keeps moving, guided by increasingly vague indi-cations. The luminous hiss of a firework, a gust of wind, autumnally sharp, coming from the Neva . . . Or else the two couples, walking along squabbling, who seem to know the route to the festivities. He is about to approach them but they get into a car, drive off . . .

He is so weary that when he comes to the Summer Garden he mistakes the high grille for yet another barrier. He grips the iron bars, his face straining towards the fragrant darkness of the pathways. The foliage is delicate, as always in this fleeting foretaste of summer. He has to force himself to concentrate so that the words dreamed of for so long can be spoken with fitting gravity: 'Beneath these very trees, thirty years ago . . .'

He hears a groan, moves away from the grille, hesitates

over what attitude to adopt. The young woman he sees appears to be drunk. Or rather . . . She has just trodden on a shard from a bottle and cut herself. The festive streets are strewn with fragments of glass. 'You need rubber boots here . . .' she moans. Shutov tells her to sit down on the ledge beside the railings, takes hold of the gashed foot, cleans the wound with the towel they gave him on the plane. The girl must be seventeen or eighteen. The age Yana was, he thinks. And he was right: she is drunk, she staggers, he needs to escort her as far as the metro. He goes down with her. The train comes so quickly they do not have time to exchange a single word. Beyond the closing doors he glimpses her sitting down, already absorbed into a life where he does not exist. And yet his hand still retains the ephemeral impression of that delicate injured foot.

He goes back to Yana's new apartment after midnight. Vlad lets him in, his ear glued to his mobile phone. The conversation is in English: the young man is talking to a client in Boston. Without breaking off he leads Shutov to the kitchen, shows him where the coffee-maker is, opens the refrigerator with a gesture of invitation, smiles, goes away.

Shutov eats, amazed by the variety of the food, the quality of the coffee. This is the kind of apartment, the type of food, which in the Soviet era the Russians used to picture when they spoke of the West . . . And here it is, they have recreated a quintessence of the West that he himself never really experienced in the West at all. A paradox which helps him to feel less behind the times.

63

He goes to look for the bedroom Yana assigned to him, gets lost, smiles. 'Why not go to sleep on the doormat, here on the threshold of this new world?' In the great bathroom the taps gleam like weighty museum pieces. 'Scythian gold . . .' he murmurs, continuing on his way.

How should he regard this new life? With delight? With regret for its frenzied materialism? After all, in ten years' time the young may well feel no feverish excitement when confronted by this intrusive stuff. Young Vlad, here, lounging on a leather sofa in front of the television. He sips a beer while on the screen, in almost the same pose, a young man embraces a blonde, whose shoulder is gradually bared in time with their sighs. A commercial break cuts short their clinch: a head of hair enriched by a particular shampoo flits by; a cat pounces upon the gleaming contents of a tin; a tall, dark, handsome man inhales his cup of coffee; a car embeds itself in a sunrise . . . Shutov remembers the slogan and mentally repeats it: 'To be on time, when every second counts!'

The old man's door is ajar. A bedside lamp, a blanket, the outline of a motionless body. And suddenly the rustle of a page. Should he go in? Speak to him, even without any hope of a reply? Or simply say goodnight? Shutov hesitates, then resumes his journey: if he starts from Vlad's office he can remember the way better.

In his bedroom he discovers what had escaped his notice earlier during the guided tour: volumes on a large wooden bookshelf painted silver. Russian and foreign classics in de luxe editions. Leather, spines with generously wide bands, gold, paper that gives sensual pleasure to the fingers. Pushkin, Gogol, Tolstoy . . . He seizes a volume of Chekhov. The story he is looking for is there. Two lovers, their descent on a toboggan. 'I love you, Nadenka . . .'

In the morning Shutov follows Yana, who talks incessantly on her mobile phone while performing a thousand useful acts: retrieving a stumbling child, pointing out the splashes of paint on the marble to the workmen in the bathroom, plugging in a kettle for breakfast, adjusting a skirt that Vlad's young girlfriend is trying on . . . Catching Shutov's eye she smiles, shakes her head by way of saying: 'I'll be with you in a second,' and the whirlwind resumes: the workmen want her opinion on the colour of a sealant, Vlad asks for money, a woman laden with a bundle of clothes proclaims that tomorrow the old man's room will be vacated. None of this prevents her from giving instructions over the telephone: 'If he needs a sitting room get number twenty-six ready . . . He ought to be perfectly happy with a standard room . . . So what? We've got fifteen ministers in our hotels. If they all started demanding suites . . . Well, let Putin put them up in his Konstantin Palace! All right, give this one a different room but not the others . . . Let me know what happens!'

Before the next call she finds time to give Shutov the name of the restaurant where they can meet for lunch and 'finally have a heart-to-heart'. The phrase is hackneyed but it touches him, he embarks on a sentence that is far too long, too nostalgic, ill-suited to the frenzied rhythm of the morning. Along the lines of: 'Do you remember that pathway through the trees in the Summer Garden?' Yana blows him a kiss and runs towards the lift, shouting into her mobile: 'It's no good here. I'll call you from the car.'

The energy of this new life is pleasantly contagious, a euphoriant drug that Shutov encounters again in the street in even stronger doses. He feels rejuvenated, almost mischievous, leaps up to catch the balloon a child has let go of, favours its mother with a wink. Buys himself an ice cream, gives directions to two young female tourists who are lost. And having reached the Nevsky Prospekt, attests to the miracle: he feels completely at one with the carnival crowd making its way towards the Winter Palace, and it is a physical belonging, a bodily adherence.

It is also a . . . face transplant! A violent image, but it expresses vividly what he feels. His new physiognomy has a skin that is regenerated by the glances alighting on him, amid a flood of smiles, shouts, embraces. Yes, a man with a skin graft must go through the same mixture of dread and delight on walking out into the street: will they notice? Turn away as I pass by? Give me pitying looks? No, it seems they perceive nothing. They all smile at this man who is not me. So I have the right to live among them once again.

At first Shutov walks along with the wariness of just such a skin-grafted man. But quite quickly the madness of what is happening all around him rids him of any fear. The music from several bands creates such a din

67

that people communicate by facial expression and gesture. Besides, the only message to be shared is one of permanent amazement. A giant inflatable cow with eight legs floats above the crowd, its enormous udder sprinkles the onlookers, who yell, dodging the jets, opening their umbrellas. A little further on the human tide is cut in half by a procession of Peter the Great lookalikes! Military frock coat, three-cornered hat, moustache like an angry cat's whiskers, cane. Most of them are of a stature at least faintly evocative of the tsar's six foot six, but there are also some little ones and even a woman dressed as the tsar. At one crossroads this regiment gets mixed up with a squad of near-naked 'Brazilian dancers', adorned with feathers. The tsars' uniforms brush against long, bronzed thighs, graze the hemispheres of plump buttocks. And quickly these give way to courtiers in periwigs, the avenue is awash with crinolines, sunlight dancing off the high, powdered coiffures. The whipped cream of their attire is succeeded by a new inflatable monster. A dinosaur? No, a ship. Shutov reads the name on its stern: *Aurora*. 'That was the cruiser in the October Revolution,' a mother explains to her son of about twelve years . . . If that historic gunshot, which children in the old days would have come across at primary school, now has to be explained, this really is a new era . . . The forgetfulness is refreshing: yes, spare them your wars and revolutions!

The loudspeakers cutting through the musical hullabaloo seem to be in agreement with Shutov: 'Welcome to the launch of the Great May Revolution. Everyone to Palace Square. The Mayor of St Petersburg is going

68

to have his head cut off.' Laughter erupts, masks scowl, another Peter the Great, this time on horseback, towers above the crowd.

And down below, almost on the ground, a shrill voice rings out: 'Let me through, I'm late! Make way!' A dwarf, an elderly man, dressed as a king's fool, or rather a tsar's fool. This waddling figure scurries along, pushing the crowd aside with his short arms. One of the 'Brazilian dancers' is with him, clearing a passage for him, shaking her feathers and her bracelets. Clearly they are expected at Palace Square and their disarray is both comic and touching. 'A buffoon,' thinks Shutov, stepping aside for the little man. 'A *shut* . . .' The half-naked dancer bumps into him, her feathers tickle his cheek, he senses the vigour of this young, perfumed body but the woman's gaze is strangely sad.

'Hey you, oaf! Why aren't you laughing like everyone else? How dare you? A head with no smile belongs on the block!' Shutov tries to break free from the hands that grip him, then yields to the game. Actors dressed as executioners surround him, he remembers the orders repeated by the loudspeakers: people with sour faces are enemies of the carnival – off with their heads! There is nothing cruel about the execution: a hilarious sentence, the swing of a plastic axe, with the crowd shouting encouragement . . . One of the executioners asks him: 'So, is it a long time since you were in St Petersburg?' but does not listen to the reply and rushes off to hunt down other resisters to the general merriment.

Once at Palace Square, Shutov begins to grasp what

lies at the heart of the changes. A geyser of energy, held in check for a long time. The frenzied search for a new logic to life after the highly logical madness of dictatorship. He sees the mayor mounting the scaffold, yes, the Mayor of St Petersburg in person! (Would this be possible in Paris or New York?) The firecrackers explode, the crowd hoots noisily, the mayor smiles, almost flattered. An executioner brandishes . . . an enormous pair of scissors, points them at the condemned man's neck, seizes his tie and cuts it off! A wave of delirium ripples across the square at the sight of the trophy displayed. A loudspeaker chokes with delight: 'A Gucci tie!' Shutov surprises himself by cheering with the others, slapping strangers' hands, physically bonded with these thousands of living beings. The little clown seen just now climbs breathlessly onto the throne and a magistrate in ceremonial robes declares him to be the governor of the city.

'A collective exorcism,' he thinks as he goes to his rendezvous with Yana. Three days of this burlesque May Revolution to undo decades of terror, to wash away the blood of real revolutions. To deafen themselves with the noise of firecrackers so as to forget the sound of bombs. To unleash these merry executioners into the streets so as to blot out the shadowy figures that came knocking at doors in the night not so long ago, dragging men out, still half asleep, throwing them into black cars.

Behind the Winter Palace a placard announces a 'family portrait'. Seated on folding chairs, a Peter the Great, a Lenin, a Stalin and, beyond an untoward gap, a Gorbachev, complete with birthmark painted on the

70

middle of his bald head. Stalin, pipe in mouth, talks on his mobile phone. A Nicholas II and a Brezhnev (the missing links) rejoin the group, laden with packs of beer. Laughter, camera flashes. The barker, a young woman in a miniskirt, moves among the crowd: 'Now then, ladies and gentlemen, spare a coin for the losers of History. We accept dollars too . . .'

'They've managed to turn the page at last,' Shutov says to himself. And the thought of being left behind, like a dried flower, between the preceding pages, gives him the desire to hurry, to catch up.

'You didn't have time to change?'

'No . . . Well, I only brought this jacket.'

'I see . . .'

Their words are drowned by the music. He smiles, ruefully, fingering the lapels of his jacket. Bulging pockets, faded material . . . The restaurant staff know Yana and greet her with respect. Some of the customers nod to her. She is among her own people, thinks Shutov, unable to guess what criterion, in the new Russia, distinguishes such people from the rest. Friendship, simply? Profession? Politics?

They sit at a terrace overlooking a park where boisterously merry music is being played, so this disturbance is not the fault of the restaurant. The head waiter offers his apologies. 'Oh, this tercentenary . . .' sighs Yana.

They need to shout to be heard but what Shutov would like to say cannot be uttered in ringing tones.

So they do as the others do, smile, eat, then yell and gesticulate. From this intermittent dialogue he learns about what he already knew: Yana's life after their brief undeclared love affair. Work, marriage, the birth of a son, divorce, return to Leningrad, which had once more become St Petersburg . . .

The words that falter within him, rendered fragile by the passage of so many years, are too frail to cut through the noise. 'Do you remember that evening at Peterhof,' he would like to say, 'the golden haze over the Gulf of Finland . . . ?' He also learns what he had not known: the hotel chain where Yana works belongs to her! Well, not to her in person, but to the mysterious 'us' she refers to when talking about her life. Her partner and her? Their family business? More than the music it is this language barrier that makes comprehension hard.

Suddenly the din stops. An amazed silence, one can hear the rustling of the leaves . . . And the mobile phones ring, as if the calls had all been waiting for this pause. No, it was simply that people could not hear them before. They all respond at the same time, delighted at having recovered the power of speech.

Yana is telephoned as well and Shutov can already manage to identify the person she is speaking to from the tone she adopts. That slightly irritated voice is directed at the staff of one of 'her' hotels. The sulky, simpering tones at a man whose bad temper has to be soothed and who seems to be a part of this vague but powerful 'us'. Her partner, no doubt. Or else a husband from whom she must conceal this lover of thirty years ago? No, that would be too stupid . . .

72

She puts the telephone aside and he hopes that at last he will be able to tell her the purpose of his visit. 'We're having a house-warming party tomorrow,' she says. 'Just a glass of champagne – it's still a building site, as you saw. There aren't even any tables. And in the evening we're inviting everyone to our country place . . . Some of the key people in St Petersburg. I don't know if you'd be interested. You won't know anyone . . . The mayor should be coming . . .' This is someone Shutov does know: the beheaded man whose Gucci tie was cut short . . .

A couple come over to greet Yana. Rapid glances of appraisal at Shutov: who is he? A Russian? But not dressed smartly enough for this spot. A foreigner? But lacking the ease of manner that can be sensed on encountering people from the West. Shutov reads this judgement in their looks. The embarrassment he had detected in Yana becomes clear to him: he is unclassifiable, difficult to introduce to friends, he has a poor social profile. When the couple move away he tries to assume the relaxed air of a former fellow student: 'So this *dacha*, where did you build it? Yes, I'd like to drop by.' Yana hesitates, as if she regrets having issued the invitation: 'It's an old *izba*. The plot is a bit constricted for us, less than eight acres. On the Gulf of Finland . . .'

A man stops in front of Yana, begins talking to her. 'The golden haze over the Gulf of Finland . . .' Shutov recalls.

The man is handsome, young (under forty, or at least at that smooth and tanned age which people with the means know how to fix). 'Tall, dark and asinine,'

73

Shutov thinks. (It was something Léa used to say and they would both laugh . . .) The malice of it makes him feel guilty. This handsome man can, in fact, be graded by American norms of virility, in such cases the French speak of B-movie heroes . . . An impeccably cut light-weight suit, the manner of a seducer indulgent towards his victims' weakness. Yana adopts a voice that is new to Shutov, an assumed nonchalance, slipping into frail tones of fond helplessness. Her face, in particular, expresses this, her eyes, as she gazes up at the man: the concerned look of a woman who has lost a loved one in the middle of a crowd. The music starts again, she stands up, draws closer to the man and this tender anxiety is even more visible when their words can no longer be heard.

'This must be her lover . . .' The brutality of the observation irritates him but he no longer has any wish to delude himself. 'The golden haze over the Gulf of Finland . . .' It was idiotic to think that she would still remember it. He calls to mind the different voices Yana employs to speak to her staff, to her husband, to this tall, dark, handsome man. She leads several lives at once and it is clear that this excites her. She stands there before her lover, considerably shorter than him, and her whole body betrays the demeanour of a woman giving herself. Shutov feels like an actor who has just missed his cue.

The man brushes Yana's cheek with his lips, takes his leave. She sits down, directs a look of radiant blindness at Shutov. They drink coffee without speaking to one another . . . As he escorts her to her car,

Shutov is tempted to warn her to go carefully, as she seems so absent. But she quickly pulls herself together, she has to 'dash off to a shareholders' meeting' and advises Shutov to return on foot, 'you take the main alley through the park and then turn left, remember.' She drives off as he embarks on an observation about how vividly he recalls those pathways amid the autumn foliage . . .

Emerging from the trees he encounters the Brazilian dancers. They are changing in a small van. Shutov recognizes the one who was running along earlier, clearing the way for the fool. She has taken off her plumage, washed away the mascara, her face is very young and her look a little melancholy, as before. Shutov perceives a tenderness in it, perhaps directed, strangely enough, towards himself . . .

As he opens the door to Yana's new apartment he hears Vlad's voice: 'Listen. It's quite simple. We need two topless girls for the back cover. Then you call the editorial team. If they won't include it in the article, we withdraw our ad and that's that . . .' Intrigued, Shutov walks towards the voice. As he passes the little bedroom where the old man lodges he catches sight of that same green blanket, a hand holding a book.

Each title includes a woman's name: *Tatyana or the Fire Tamer*; *Deborah and the Chemistry of Pleasure*; *Bella, a Woman with No Taboos* . . . Vlad is showing Shutov the new series launched by his publishing house. They lifted the idea from Nabokov's *Ada or Ardor*, he concedes. But Nabokov himself borrowed it from women's romantic fiction . . . The young man talks a language Shutov has never heard in Russia. 'Market analysis', 'book promotion', 'boosting sales' . . . For the new series what they needed was a clear definition of the 'generational niche', which, happily, is quite broad: female readers between the ages of thirty and fifty who are 'not very intellectual' (coming from Vlad, this is a compliment) and a small minority of men who 'have a bit of a problem with sex' and will read these books on the quiet.

Seeing Shutov's perplexed expression, Vlad hastens to add: 'Fine, we also have more serious brands!' and he mentions various series of historical novels, family sagas, political fiction . . . But it is the word 'brand' that disconcerts Shutov. Vlad translates: 'They're . . . how do you say it in Russian? Well . . . Yes. Makes, labels. You see, all these Bellas and Tatyanas, we have to bring them out at regular intervals. That's how you create reading habits, you know, get people addicted. The problem is that each of these books runs to five hundred pages. No writer can keep pace with that. Unless he's what my grandfather used to call a Stakhanovite. And so several of them write under one name, preferably an American one. That's a brand . . .'

Vlad notices that this explanation plunges Shutov even deeper into thought. He leans over, picks up several volumes that are lying there on the wall-to-wall carpet. 'Look, there's some heavyweight stuff as well.' Shutov scans the titles. *Secrets of the Kremlin*; *Stalin, Between God and the Devil*; *Nicholas II, the Innocence of a Martyr* . . .

'Are you sure he was really innocent?' asks Shutov, trying to rouse himself from his bemusement.

'Of course. They've just made him a saint!'

'For having led Russia into revolution . . .'

'No, hold on. The revolution was a plot hatched abroad. Look, this book here is quite categorical about it . . .'

Menacing shadows on a blood-red cover. *The Occult Forces Behind the Revolution*. Shutov smiles.

'Ouch! That's scary!'

'That's the idea. And you should have seen the ad I put together for the launch. There was this Russian monk praying in front of an icon with a crowd of devils dancing all around him . . .'

'That's not very close to the historical truth. Especially if your monk looked like Rasputin.'

'Historians rewrite the truth every day. What interests us is the truth that gets the reader to reach for

77

his wallet. You know what my boss's motto is? "Only the blind are excused from buying our books." And it's more or less the case. But you need imagination for it. When we were launching the book on Stalin I dug up a cleaning woman who'd worked at his *dacha* on the Black Sea. Imagine that! She's a granny aged a hundred now, but I still managed to get her on TV and the interviewer (well, he's one of our authors) questioned her in such a way that you might have thought she'd been Stalin's mistress. The next day we'd sold out. That's historical truth. Or take *Bella with No Taboos*. It talks about a brothel where the Moscow underworld go. Well, to launch it on TV we had five prostitutes who swore everything in the book was true . . .'

Vlad gets carried away, soon Shutov has not enough arms to hold the rolls of posters, the large-format photographs: Nicholas II adorned with the halo of a newly canonized saint; Stalin with a female figure in the background and a gangster thrusting open the collar of a blouse with the barrel of his revolver to reveal enormous, very pink breasts.

'The same carnival yet again,' thinks Shutov, violently struck once more by the heady intoxication of the change. What energy this young Vlad has! And this easy-going cynicism, selling books like vacuum cleaners. All these publishing houses have sprung up in just a few years! And already they have this American-style know-how . . .

Suddenly, in the armful of documents, Shutov catches sight of a view of a park, with sculptures beneath autumnal foliage. The Summer Garden . . . The picture

78

vanishes beneath a swatch of colour photographs: women embracing, men exchanging tender kisses . . .

'That's our series aimed at sexual minorities,' comments Vlad. 'I told you. No one escapes us!' He laughs.

Shutov remembers the carnival executioners who cut off his head earlier: that's it, no one is to look sad. The parallel is disturbing.

'You know, Vlad, in the old days, when I was young, a good many poets were published. The print runs for their books were not vast but there was . . . How can I put it? . . . Yes, there was real passion in those of us who read them. Often printed on very poor paper. Poetry was our Bible . . .'

'Yeah, I can see what kind of books you're talking about. The old folks heave a sigh and call it "Great Literature". Listen, I'll tell you what I think about it. I once met a girl, an American in the same job as me. And she started giving me a lot of stuff, like: oh sure, we publish crap but that's so we can publish Real Literature! What two-faced bastards these puritans are! Well, I wanted to put her on the spot so I quoted Marx: the only criterion of truth is the practical result. And in publishing the result is the number of sales, okay? If crap books sell it's because they're needed. You should have seen her face!'

He roars with laughter, then glancing at the television declares: 'But the main thing is, if I published your poets with their small print runs, I'd never be able to afford wheels like that.'

On the screen (the sound is off) the car races up

towards the sunrise. 'To be on time, when every second counts!' Vlad's mobile phone emits jazz notes and the conversation breaks into slangy English, incomprehensible to Shutov. Vlad covers the telephone with his hand, winks at Shutov and whispers: 'Only joking!' Yes, only a joke, that remark about the car, thinks Shutov, as he puts aside the rafts of photographs piled up in his lap. A joke, *shutka*, the same root as his name . . .

Behind the door where the mute old man lodges, the chink of a spoon against a cup can be heard.

Shutov makes his way back to his room, his halting steps keeping pace with the arguments that jostle one another in his head. Wisdom after the event . . . He should have told Vlad that in the old days a collection of poems could change your life but a single poem could also cost the life of its author. Lines of verse carried the weight of long sentences north of the arctic circle where so many poets died . . .

He imagines Vlad's mocking reply: 'And you think that was good?' There it is. A naive question like this is hard to counter. Why should the Gulag be a criterion of good literature? And suffering a measure of authenticity? But, above all, who can judge the value of lives, of books? In what way can Vlad's existence be said to be less meaningful than that of some poor sod using his last few kopecks to buy a pamphlet by a banned poet printed on wrapping paper? To these young Russians no book is forbidden now. They travel the world (Vlad has just come back from Boston), they are well fed, well educated, free of complexes . . . And yet they lack something . . .

Shutov is trying not to think like a petty, embittered old man. No, Vlad has no reason to be jealous of that Soviet youth of thirty years ago. They had nothing to set him dreaming. Nothing. Except, perhaps, a volume of poems with greyish pages, verses aglow with the golden light of leaves in a park . . . 'I should have told him,' thinks Shutov and knows he could not have found the right words: a verbal block that makes him unable to explain the richness of that wretched past.

He opens the window, hears sounds in the background suggestive of a carnival grown weary, a gaiety running out of steam, sustained by dint of street performances now stagnating into pools of noise. Outside couples and groups of friends are passing. A far-fetched but tempting notion occurs to him. To go down and confide in them. 'I've just come out of a coma lasting twenty years. I don't understand anything. Explain it to me!' He smiles, closes the window again and with nervous wariness switches on a large flat-screen television. The sound is deafening – several seconds of panic before he masters the remote control. And a resigned realization: this house is full of objects he will never learn to use properly.

On the screen is a thoroughbred dog, with a long, haughty, nervous muzzle. Hands with varnished nails fasten a glittering collar about the animal's neck. A figure appears: 14,500. Fourteen thousand five hundred dollars, the presenter confirms, and specifies the various precious stones which decorate this accoutrement. A sequence of other models: rubies, topazes, diamonds . . . The numbers lengthen to match the rarity of the gems. The next scene features a dog with clipped hair, whose body, sensitive to the cold, is to benefit from a distinctive garment. Fox fur, beaver or sable capes . . .

The same range of furs for its ankle boots . . . The programme now moves on to a more difficult species to domesticate. A lynx, which must undergo a pedicure if you care about your carpets and furniture. A vet is seen filing down the animal's claws . . . For a dwarf hippopotamus, whose well-being depends on a good level of humidity, the installation of a hygrometer is essential. The brightness of the colours on your python's skin can be enhanced by a wide range of food supplements . . .

Shutov feels anger mounting within him but the programme is more subtle than he thought. This feature about the pets of the new rich is supplemented by a debate between two commentators (one for, one against) with interventions from the audience. 'No one escapes us!' Shutov remembers. The less well-heeled members of the audience fulminate and one of the commentators sides with them. The affluent approve and the second commentator defends them. At the end a compromise emerges: if there are madmen willing to buy diamonds for their doggies let them go ahead, this is a democracy. Shutov realizes that he was not far off thinking this himself, so his fury did not make much sense. New wealth makes such extravagances possible and it would be naive to invoke who knows what moral principle to condemn them.

What a fantastic device for lobotomizing us, he reflects, hopping from one channel to another. The mind is chloroformed, the rebellious spirit is tamed. Every opinion is present. A procession of orthodox priests files into a cathedral: the Greeks have brought the relics of

83

Saint Andrei for the tercentenary. And on the very next channel two young lesbian rock singers are explaining that in London they had to 'tone down' their concert because European audiences are too prudish. The 'non-toned-down' version shows them sitting one on top of the other, massaging their crotches and howling into their mikes . . . A night scene: young men with shaven heads, Nazi salutes . . . An American sitcom: three idiots, two white, one black, saying stupid things to one another, intercut with canned laughter . . . More dogs, this time without diamonds; they are searching for explosives at the Kirov Theatre, where the forty-five heads of state invited for the celebration will gather. A football match. An English great-nephew of Nicholas II arriving at St Petersburg in a vintage car. An erotic film – the cries of pleasure in Russian are reminiscent of the instructions for a domestic appliance. VIP guests in front of the equestrian statue of Peter the Great; it is raining, Blair shelters his wife under an umbrella, Putin is stoical, Chirac arrives at the double, having been held up at the Hermitage (the commentator explains) by his interest in antiques . . . Another football match. 'To be on time, when every second . . .' Sequences in black and white: archives from the Second World War, Stalin on a platform, columns of soldiers setting off to defend Moscow. An interview with Madame Putin: 'Women should choose personal dressmakers. This would save them from encountering guests at receptions wearing the same Yves Saint Laurent gown as themselves . . .' Reportage from the Summer Garden where eighteenth-century courtiers are strolling, wigs, crinolines, lorgnettes . . .

Shutov gets up, he has just recognized the corner of a pathway in the park, a statue . . . Nothing has changed in thirty years. And everything has changed. The meaning of the transformation appears clear to him. Russia is attempting to erase the decades that came between her and her destiny: several of Vlad's books spoke of this Russian destiny, interrupted by the disastrous Soviet digression. Yes, a beautiful river polluted by the sludge of massacres, intellectual slavery, fear. 'And the truth is that young Vlad is closer to those crinolines than he is to the phantom of the USSR. He has more in common with Nicholas II's English great-nephew than with a Soviet dinosaur like me . . .' Shutov smiles but the perception is painful: over his head History is returning to its course, becoming more limpid . . . while he remains mired in those accursed times everyone would prefer to forget.

'I was wrong to come . . .' he tells himself. But has he really arrived anywhere? A journey from an attic in a block of flats in Paris, where he felt so little at home, to this luxury apartment, where he is even more of a stranger. 'I came to see Yana again . . .' He glances at the clock on the television. Ten thirty p.m. At the restaurant Yana had promised to call for him at about eight.

He goes down into the street, into that pale luminescence of northern nights and begins to walk with a resolute tread, and a feeling that he is staking everything on one last throw of the dice.

The Hermitage is open all night, it was announced on television. He goes there, is glad to mingle with the

85

throng crowding in at the entrance, laughs at the quip repeated by several voices: 'So here we go, storming the Winter Palace again!' The memory of the carnival comes back to him, the tribal warmth, the hope of renewing links with that world on which he is twenty years in arrears. He will catch someone's eye in front of a painting, strike up a conversation . . .

From his first steps inside he freezes, dumbfounded. The atmosphere is reminiscent of a railway station. People sitting on the floor, leaning against the wall, some of them asleep. Others, perched on the window ledges, are scanning the sky: a son et lumière spectacle above the Neva has been promised. Two adolescents stretched out behind a gigantic malachite vase are idly kissing. A tourist in shorts speaks very loudly in German to a female companion, clad in the same brand of shorts (but three times as wide) who nods as she bites into a thick sandwich. A group of Asians passes by, filming every picture in the room with highly disciplined synchronization. A husband explains to his wife: 'The metro opens again at five. We might as well spend the night here.' Ladies in crinolines and moustached hussars materialize, like ghosts, in imitation of the ones who used to frequent the palace. But the crowd is too tired to pay them any attention.

Shutov walks on, observes, and his thoughts about Russia returning to the brilliant high road of her destiny seem to have been too hasty. For there is also a confusion of styles, the disappearance of a way of life and barely the first babblings of a new manner of being . . . In front of a glass case a little girl is laughing at the exhibits. He pricks up his ears and realizes that the chuckling of this child is, in fact, almost silent sobbing. She has lost her parents in a room where there's a 'big pot'. He is about to alert an attendant then guesses that the big pot must be that malachite vase. They go to it and the child recognizes its parents: that young couple locked in an embrace whom Shutov took to be teenage sweethearts . . . As he leaves the child, he thinks he has surprised in its look the pained incomprehension he feels himself.

He walks out of the museum and allows himself to be sucked in by the throng. Thousands of people, like a sponge ever more tightly squeezed, are waiting for the sky to be set ablaze by the spotlights of a Japanese artist. New arrivals add to the pressure, the most agile climb trees. 'Three million dollars, that's what it's going to cost us!' a voice proclaims and a chorus responds with the sum total of the artist's fees. The night is not dark enough for the luminous fantasies to materialize. The clouds light up but the wind from the Neva tears them apart instantly. The people rail wearily against the Japanese and begin to disperse.

All that remains of the jubilant enthusiasm for the carnival is this indifferent clustering of the crowd as it moves from place to place in search of the last stray sparks of the festival. On Palace Square Shutov listens to the performance of a former dissident singer. A familiar repertoire: camps, prisons, blood. The human mass laughs, yawns, moves off and spills into the Nevsky Prospekt. There it divides up; Shutov is carried along by a section retracing its footsteps. He does not notice the precise moment when what he observes switches into a fantastic dreamscape. Perhaps when a batrachian figure breaks the surface of a canal: frogmen are checking the place where tomorrow the procession of the masters of the world is due to pass. Or else when the smell of urine invading the streets becomes intolerable. 'Silks for fine ladies at their toilet,' jokes an elderly man. 'But no toilets for the people.' At the English Embankment the crowd is turned aside by a police cordon: a cruise ship is moored there, the floating hotel for the presidents of the former Soviet republics. 'Nine suites at six thousand dollars a night,' a woman announces in bizarrely gleeful tones. 'I read that in the paper.' Her partner hugs her tightly. 'It's a disgrace,' he retorts. 'That's what you get in a year. And look at Bush. He's taken over the whole of the Astoria Hotel . . .'

The rain gets heavier, breaks up the crowd into narrower trickles. One of these expels Shutov onto the edge of the Field of Mars. He crosses the esplanade where groups of young people are hanging about. They are drinking, throwing empty bottles, scuffling, leaping over the flame in the monument to the dead. One of them unbuttons himself to urinate into the fire. Shutov tries to reprimand him but his voice is lost amid the shouting. This saves him, for those who heard him are already bearing down on him, he can hear oaths, almost good-natured in their mockery: 'Hey, old man. Do you want your bollocks fried or roasted?' He edges away, trying to slow his pace so as not to betray the humiliating fear stiffening his back.

But what saves him is the final coda to this nocturnal phantasmagoria: they start raising the bridges over the Neva and he is forced to hurry, making long detours to avoid the trap of the now disunited islands.

Catching sight of his own distraught face in the lift, Shutov concludes with philosophical gravity: 'I think I understand it all now.' He does not know whom he is trying to convince, but the lie helps him to hold back his tears.

Vlad greets him with exaggerated benevolence. 'I've prepared stuff for your supper. There's smoked sturgeon, unless you'd rather . . . And there's wine, but you're probably choosy on that front, like all the French . . . Ma called. Unfortunately she wasn't able to get away . . . There's also some Far Eastern crab . . . So how was St Petersburg by night?'

His warm friendliness moves Shutov. A man with his back to the wall can feel choked by emotion. Why not make a clean breast of it? This abortive trip, the failed reunion with Yana . . . He sits down at the table in the kitchen (a place of long sleepless nights for Russians of his generation, during which things both spiritual and spirituous were shared) and begins talking. The crinolines in the Summer Garden, the city as it used to be, so far from festive and yet . . .

He quickly notices that the young man is not listening. Vlad stands there glancing discreetly at his watch, then finally, unable to hold out any longer, ventures: 'Let's talk about it tomorrow, if you like. We'll have all the time in the world . . . The thing is . . . I did have a favour to ask you . . . You see, I've been working at home for the past four days and it's not easy . . .' Shutov supposes that Vlad is after some advice linked to his profession, his opinion on an author, on a translation . . . He even has time to feel important, endowed with great literary experience . . . And then the nature of the request becomes clear.

'The truth is, if I'm hanging around here it's on account of the old man. Ma is terrified that something might happen to him just before the move . . .' Vlad lowers his voice: 'It's not so much that he might kick the bucket. That's manageable, we call a doctor, he makes a report and *hasta la vista!* No, what would be more serious would be . . . you see, he's dumb. Who knows what's going on in his head? Just imagine if he cut his own throat. He's got a perfectly good pair of hands, he could do it. They might accuse us of maltreating him and who knows what besides. Especially as my stepfather has a very public position! Ma's worried. I help her as much as I can. It's just that . . . Since I got back from the States I've seen nothing of my . . . girlfriend. Okay, she did come in this morning to try on the clothes I brought back for her. But with that whole crowd milling around here, it wasn't very private . . .'

Shutov was part of 'that whole crowd' himself. Vlad hastens to clarify. 'We can't really kiss one another under the nose of a grandpa! You see, here we are in the middle of these celebrations and I've got to look after an ancient ruin! So I'm watching the carnival on TV. It's worse than being in jail. Then my girlfriend called me. She came straight out with it: "You choose.

It's either me or that old basket case!" Sure, women always go over the top . . . But that's how things stand. So I wanted to ask you a big favour. If you could stay with the old man until morning . . . I promise, on my honour, at half past six I'll take over from you and at eight o'clock the medics will be collecting him . . . Are you sure? That wouldn't be a problem for you?'

Shutov reassures him, mentions the time difference. ('In Paris I go to bed at two a.m., which is to say four a.m. here . . .') Vlad stammers out his thanks, gives some instructions: 'He's already had his ration of food, so that's done. Now if you see his pot's full . . . But he doesn't urinate much. Listen, I'll be in your debt for life! When you're back in St Petersburg next time, don't hesitate . . .'

The door bangs shut and out on the landing the young man's voice can be heard yelling the good news to his girlfriend into a mobile phone.

The television opposite Vlad's office is showing an opera (the eyes of the forty-five heads of state staring at the beads of sweat on Pavarotti's brow). Through the half-open door to the bedroom can be seen a green blanket, a hand holding a book. From time to time the rustle of a page can be heard.

Shutov laughs, chuckling inwardly at first, then, recalling that the old man is doubtless deaf as well as dumb, stops holding back, his chest shaking with an attack of hilarity. The wistful beauty of the reunion he planned is toppling over into burlesque. Having come as a nostalgic pilgrim, he finds himself surrounded by modernity gone mad, a mixture of American razzle-dazzle and Russian clowning. He has sought to understand this new country and they reject him, along with the worn-out relics of Soviet times, in the company of a bedridden deaf-mute, whose chamber pot he will have to empty.

He laughs, aware that this is the only way he can avoid lapsing into emotionalism over that lost paradise. His childhood at the orphanage, a paradise? Or his impoverished youth, perhaps? Or the history of this country, written between two lines of barbed wire? No, no, let's laugh about it, for fear of weeping. Occasions for uproarious laughter are not lacking. On the screen Pavarotti's stentorian rotundity is now abandoned by the camera as it focuses on quite a different vocalist, Berlusconi, who is singing along with half-closed eyes, while Putin casts amused glances at him. Shutov changes channels. A feature on the parade of old tramcars. When the Nazis laid siege to Leningrad these vehicles were used to transport the corpses of those citizens who had starved to death. Shutov surfs the channels: an Indian film, a woman in raptures, a man on a smart motorbike crushes his enemy. CNN: the stock market is rising, a general talks about restoring peace. The Russian equivalent of CNN and the wonder of these endlessly repeated news items: Madame Putin once more urging women to choose a personal dress-maker, the Greeks yet again handing over the relics of Saint Andrei, and the two female rock singers complaining about the excessive prudery of British audiences . . . And when, switching to another channel,

Shutov hits upon the same erotic film, the position of the bodies creates the illusion that their coupling has been going on uninterrupted for many hours. The commercial for tinned cat food. A biker hastens to wash his 'dull and tired' hair with nourishing shampoo. A car hurtles towards the sun: 'To be on time, when every second counts!' An executioner snips the St Petersburg mayor's tie. An obese young black man in an American sitcom has two slightly idiotic young white men in stitches. In a Baltic state a parade of former SS men. A shaving-cream commercial . . .

Shutov eats in front of the television (the wine is good, even for a 'choosy' Frenchman) and he feels almost happy. Relaxed, at least, thanks to the absurdities flooding the screen. The secret he sought to fathom is simple: Russia has just caught up with the global game of role-playing, its antics, its codes. And the tercentenary celebrations only sharpen this impetus towards the great world spectacular: forty-five heads of state stuffed with our caviar, glutted with our vodka, bored with our Tchaikovsky. Bill Gates and his riches? Better to admire our own millionaires, who have achieved this status in just a few years!

The two presenters who were earlier commenting on the animal fads of the new rich appear on the screen again. They are talking now about the holidays these tycoons treat themselves to: a pleasure yacht three hundred feet long, with a helicopter and a pocket submarine on board and a gold-plated swimming pool, which, during parties for friends, is filled with champagne. The reporters disagree over the make and the year . . . Another click and an old tram can be seen crossing the starving city during the war.

Shutov's laughter subsides into a relieved sigh. No point in cudgelling one's brains, just accept the world carnival which the Russians have now joined. All aboard! The merry-go-round revolves and only pre-historic creatures like him still care about the previous century. Nostalgists dreaming of evening mists over the Baltic Sea, while the global merry-go-round, as it gathers speed, hurls them away to bite the dust amid the nettles, far from the carnival.

From the old man's bedroom comes a dull coughing, then the rustle of a page. Shutov glances in through the half-open door, remembers about the chamber pot, is it time already? Go and say goodnight to him? Spend a moment beside him? This human presence, at once mute and filled with grave sense, makes him ill at ease.

'It's because we're from the same era . . .' An un-attractive notion, Shutov tries to qualify it. No, it's more than that, this old man is a whole era on his own. According to Yana's account, the life whose shadow lies huddled beneath the green blanket can easily be imagined. In his youth this man sang in one of the choirs that often went to the front to support the soldiers. Trenches on a plain swept by snow, a stage put together from ammunition boxes, singers concealing their shiv-ering, laughing, performing a medley of classics. After that . . . What could have become of him? The same as everyone else: with Leningrad under siege, able-bodied men found themselves out on those icy plains. Then the

94

years of a slow advance on Berlin, which, if Yana is to be believed, was where he ended his war. And then what? Rebuilding the country, marriage, children, work, routine, old age . . . A banal life. But also an extra-ordinary one. This same man, as a youth, in a city which Hitler planned to turn into a vast desert. Two and a half years of siege, more than a million victims, which is to say a small township wiped out every day. Bitterly harsh winters, death lying in wait in the dark labyrinths of the streets, an ice megalopolis without bread, without heat, without transport. Flats populated by corpses. Incessant bombing. And theatres continuing to put on performances, people going to them after working fourteen hours in arms factories . . . In the old days at school they used to learn the history of that city bled white, which stood its ground.

The old man coughs in his bedroom, then the scrape of a cup can be heard as he sets it down on his bedside table. What is one to think of his life? Shutov fails to silence conflicting voices within himself. A heroic life? Yes, but also one quite stupidly sacrificed. Fine, doubt-less, in its self-denial. And absurd because the country for which he fought no longer exists. Tomorrow this old man will find himself in some humdrum provincial poorhouse in the company of forsaken invalids, surrounded by nurses who steal everything there is in the home to be stolen. What a glorious end!

Another rustle of a page. Shutov feels a prickle of anger. In his youth he saw too much of this fatalistic Russian resignation. Yes, tomorrow the old man will be thrown out, but this does not stop him clinging to

95

his cup of cold tea, his book with its yellowed pages. They promised him paradise on earth, they ruined the best years of his life, they made him live in this dump as crowded as a commuter train. He did not flinch. He simply lost the use of his legs and his tongue. So as not to be tempted to protest, no doubt. They pay him a monthly pension equal to the tip Yana's friends leave the waiter in a night club. He does not even grumble. He reads. Makes no demands, uncomplaining, uncritical of the new life that will spring up out of his remains. Yes, this life Shutov can see on television: gold-painted performers prancing about in front of the forty-five heads of state when they go off to dine in the Throne Room . . . But is he aware of this life? Perhaps, if he could see it, might he not emit one of those protracted cries that dumb people are capable of, a mixture of indignation and pain? Yes, he must see it!

Shutov acts without leaving himself time to think. Unplugs the television, pushes it towards the old man's bedroom, nudges open the door with his shoulder, places the set at the foot of the bed, plugs it in again. And settles down a little way off, so as to observe the reactions of this strange viewer.

The man does not seem to be particularly surprised. He removes his glasses and focuses a severely tranquil gaze on Shutov, which mellows into indifference. His big hand covers the book he has just closed. His eyes stare at the screen without hostility but also without curiosity.

Shutov begins channel-hopping. The old man's face

appears just as neutral as at the start. Nicholas II's English great-nephew arrives in St Petersburg, the Greek priests process with their relics, two lesbian rock singers complain of the English being too prudish, Berlusconi sings his duet with Pavarotti, a Russian oligarch buys himself six chalets in the Alps . . . No particular expression appears on that old face, with its sunken eye sockets, its massive straight nose. 'He must be deaf . . .' Shutov says to himself, but the eyes staring at the screen are those of someone who hears and understands.

The surrealist folly of the spectacle ought to bring grimaces to this old mask focused on the television. First comes a beautiful greyhound, with all the curvature of its pedigree, which its master, to amuse his guests, regales with a dish of caviar. No, the features of the mask are impassive. To keep the clouds away during the celebrations the town hall spent a million dollars . . . The mask remains rigid. Chancellor Schröder, arm in arm with Putin, inaugurates the Amber Room at the Peterhof Palace, in the township once razed to the ground by the Nazis. Shutov peers to see if the mask will show any bitterness, any trace of rancour. Nothing. 'Women,' says Madame Putin, 'should go to a personal dressmaker for their wardrobe.' An ancient tram that carried the dead during the blockade of Leningrad . . . The old man's gaze sharpens, as if he can see beyond what is visible to today's viewers.

Shots of the carnival. An erotic film. CNN: Bush landing by helicopter. A programme devoted to the tercentenary, a survivor of the blockade recalls the daily ration: a hundred and twenty-five grams of bread. An orthodox priest relates how, in the darkest days of the siege, a procession passed round the city three times, carrying the icon of Our Lady of Kazan, and Leningrad did not fall . . .

The mask acquires a faint line of severity. Shutov seems to be entering into communication with the silent man.

A football match. The cruise ship *Silver Whisper*, with its nine presidential suites. Two female rock singers perched on top of one another. At the Mariinsky Theatre the soprano Renée Fleming is singing Tatyana in *Eugene Onegin* . . .

The mask wavers and at once closes up again, retreats into its solitude. The show goes on. The ladies in crinolines pass through the galleries at the Hermitage. Fireworks at the Peterhof. Putin shakes Paul McCartney's hand after a performance in Moscow on Red Square. 'Your songs, Paul, have always been a breath of freedom for us . . .'

Absurdity has reached its limits, thinks Shutov. He again hits upon the programme about the lives of the new rich and no longer takes the trouble to switch channels. The two presenters are visiting a show house on an estate under construction close to St Petersburg. 'High security', 'luxury homes', 'top-quality materials' . . . Language evocative of this grotesque social climbing, higher, ever higher, towards the best place in the sun.

Shutov begins to doze off. This paradise from which simple mortals are excluded is less outrageous than dogs lapping up caviar. Villas crammed with electronics but, after all, the rich have to live somewhere. Each dwelling will have a name, there will be an 'Excelsior', a 'Capitol' . . . The two presenters emerge from 'Buckingham' and set about describing the beauties of gardens in the English style . . . 'And in the greenhouses, you'll be harvesting pineapples and guavas . . .'

'That's exactly the place where we were fighting to the death. For the motherland, as we used to say in those days . . .'

Shutov gives a start, the remark is too unusual to have come from the mouth of one of the presenters. Besides, they are still singing the praises of the gardens. He looks at the old man. The same mask, the same calm eyes. Suddenly his lips move: 'Yes, there. That river, the Lukhta. They had to cross it under heavy fire . . .'

Shutov is speechless, turning over in his mind what he has just heard: 'We were fighting . . . for the motherland.' The words came out with no rhetorical flourish, there was even an ironic hesitation, acknowledging the naivety of the time-honoured expression. But that last remark, which he saw forming on the old man's lips, was neutral, the name of a river, a topographical fact. Shutov clears his throat and speaks as if he were the one recovering the power of speech: 'Forgive me . . . I . . . I thought . . . Well, in fact, they told me you couldn't . . .' The old man turns his head, changes his position to look at Shutov. 'Yes, they told me that you were . . . dumb. That you had lost . . . er . . . the power of speech.'

The old man smiles.

'You can see that's not so.'

'But then, why . . . have you never spoken to anyone?'

99

'Spoken about what?'

'I don't know . . . Life . . . Yes, this new life.'

And this, too!

On the screen a kennel can be seen adjoining the show house; the presenter is explaining about the air-conditioning system as a large white greyhound rubs against his leg.

'Well, what's to be said about it? Everything's clear these days.'

He falls silent and Shutov is gripped by an irrational fear: what if the old man should relapse into terminal mutism! The programme shows workmen felling a tree: the shrill whine of the trunk being sawn, the crash of the branches.

'Yes. That's where we were fighting. And with no help from any icons either . . . Let me introduce myself. The name's Volsky, Georgy Lvovich.'

III

On 21 June 1941 at the Nord Café, which was very popular with the people of Leningrad, Volsky lived through the last hours of his old life, the last day of peace, without knowing it. A moment of bliss, epitomized by the taste of a cup of hot chocolate.

A young woman with dark brown hair had joined this group of friends who, like him, were students at the Conservatoire. She was eating a pastry, a trace of cream remained on her lips, a moustache that made everyone laugh . . . Volsky spoke to her, their conversation became detached from the hubbub in the room. He lived in the same district as her and it pleased him greatly to remark: 'It's a small world and yet we've never met before . . .' Simple words that helped him to grasp with fresh intensity what it was he had become. From being a penniless provincial he had been transformed into a young singer, speaking on equal terms to a young woman of good family from Leningrad. They agreed to meet again, a hint of a reunion that promised a glorious day very soon.

This was the moment when the taste of hot chocolate became associated with the future life he dreamed of. A peasant's son, he had managed, not without some gritting of teeth, to win recognition for his talent, to gain acceptance, armed only with his voice. His future was like the overture to an opera; he often pictured himself at the Kirov Theatre, in *Rigoletto* or *Boris Godunov*.

From his childhood he retained the memory of those hands, his father's and mother's, lined palms, encrusted with earth. His arrival in Leningrad had wrenched him away from the gravitational pull of his origins, liberating his footsteps from the mud of country roads, allowing him to run, to escape . . . He would live in the weightlessness of song, he thought. Just as others lived from the harsh weight of physical labour. He was sufficiently pleased with himself to justify this dispensation and to declare himself the winner. A conqueror who would collude with the proudest city in Russia, and win acclaim from beautiful women with eyes that shone in the darkness of boxes at the theatre.

Such thoughts were mingled that evening with the clear light of a late sunset, the laughter of his friends in the café's great hall, and the taste of hot chocolate drunk in little sips.

The next day the loudspeaker attached to a post opposite the Nord Café was to announce the start of the war. As did thousands of other loudspeakers from the Black Sea to the Pacific.

In the very same street in September he saw a block of flats where the front had just been ripped out by bombing. The insides of the dwellings, almost undamaged, astonished him more than the totally demolished

104

buildings, already numerous in the besieged city. In an armchair at the far end of a room on the first floor Volsky could make out a body, a motionless face . . . He hastened to think back to that evening of 21 June, the taste of hot chocolate.

The same memory returned one morning in October: a woman slipped over on the frozen bank of the Neva and he rushed to her aid, caught the bucket she was trying to fill. In the flats the water had been cut off for weeks but this was when he became aware of the strangeness of the situation. A modern metropolis in which people drew water from the river and drank the murky liquid. He thought again about that cup of hot chocolate.

He recalled it, too, that night when, in the entrance hall to his block of flats, he heard a child's voice, a whine similar to the groaning of a drunkard. He climbed the staircase, feeling his way, accustomed to living without electricity, and the moaning came closer, now forming into words, then stopped all at once. He struck a match (a priceless treasure) and saw, at his feet, an old man's head upon the slender body of a little boy. The flame went out, he gave a call at the doorway to a flat. A rustling could be heard, no voice. 'Wait here,' he said to the child, invisible in the darkness. 'I'll come back. I'll give you something to eat.' He brought what people fed on in the besieged city: a slab of bread made partly from straw. A burning block of wood from the floor served as a torch to light his path. The child was no longer there. The door to one of the flats remained open. Volsky peered in and gave a shout, but did not have the courage to venture into the cold caverns of the rooms . . .

Back at his own place, he devoured the bread as if someone had tried to snatch it from him. Then remained for a long while in the darkness, picturing the child in a labyrinth of rooms where it had become possible to come across a corpse. Now he grasped that it was not hunger driving him to return to the night of 21 June and his cup of hot chocolate. It was distress, rather, at seeing how the city's death throes were becoming routine. And how he was quickly slipping into a way of life where one went to sleep at night without worrying about a starving child dying in a neighbouring flat . . .

He blew furiously on the embers at the bottom of a small metal basin transformed into a stove, and threw in several strips of wood levered up from the floor. Closed his eyes. The wave of warmth had the feel of a summer's evening . . . The Nord Café, the laughter of his friends, gathered there after a rehearsal. One of them amuses himself by giving voice to everything they say in song, as in an operatic aria. A girl acquires a moustache by biting into a pastry, blushes, and Volsky, noticing that she is beautiful, blushes as well. Amid the laughter he learns her name: Mila.

He awoke hearing the high-pitched note of a stringed instrument. The sound came from the corridor of the communal flat, from the room occupied by an old couple. These neighbours no longer got out of bed and when they needed help, one of them would scrape the strings of an old violin . . . He picked up the can of water that was heating on the stove, the sounds guiding him in the darkness. He told himself he must find the child and take him to the old people's room, closer to this source of sound that could be life-saving.

The next day as he consulted the thermometer behind its glass window (twenty-seven below), he became aware of an echo of past happiness within himself: a skating rink, fleeting silhouettes, a loudspeaker pouring forth waltzes and tangos . . . At present the falling of this fine red line meant only one thing: an increase in the stiffening of people's bodies.

That morning was a milestone in the history of the besieged city. The bread ration was reduced to a hundred and twenty-five grams per person. A week before, the warehouses containing reserves of food had been bombed and in the fire the supplies that could have fed the population of two million for a month had gone up in flames. The word 'blockade' rang out now like a death sentence: the garrotte of encirclement, no link with the outside world, no hope of survival. A slice of bread per day, exhaustion, immobility, nothingness. Those who could pick up Western radio stations learned of Hitler's decision: the city, soon to be occupied, would not be emptied of its inhabitants, they would remain there, cut off from the world, without food, without water, without medical care and, at the end of the winter, the army of the Reich would undertake 'operations of sanitary maintenance', that is to say the destruction of two million corpses. The people of Leningrad said to themselves that this project was already under way.

Volsky ate his bread ration between bombing raids. With three other young men he had just been making his way across the roofs of several buildings where they picked up incendiary bombs, rendering them harmless with the aid of enormous steel tongs. Silence returned, he sat down behind a skylight to shelter from the wind, took out his bread, and chewed it for a long time to outwit his hunger. His gaze took in the lines of the main avenues, the spire of the Cathedral of Peter and Paul and that of the Admiralty. On the promontory of Vasilievsky Island, opposite the Winter Palace, the anti-aircraft guns pointed their long barrels into the sky. Some of the monuments were hidden beneath a casing of planks as protection against shells. The Neva extended out into a broad snow-covered plain. The day was clear, blue, more beautiful than ever, thanks to the absence of traffic and crowds. A magnificent shroud, thought Volsky. Yes, a vast graveyard filled with buildings where, day after day, thousands of hearts ceased beating. No other life was possible.

The future life he had dreamed of flitted past in his mind, like a speeded-up theatrical performance: sparkling lights, operatic arias hummed to the rhythm of vaude-ville chorus songs, frenzied applause . . . It still seemed incredibly close. And already hopeless, ludicrous.

He went back to his comrades who were walking along the roof. Sparing movements, sluggish gestures. One might have thought that this slowness was due to fear of slipping. No, it was how people fed on a hundred and twenty-five grams of bread a day moved. Never-theless they kept going through the cold, through days

108

that all presaged the end. Through the only life that remained to them, one far too much like death . . . One after another, they came down into the attics, then, via an iron ladder, onto the top floor of the building. On the threshold of a flat stood a woman with a child in her arms. She greeted them with a faint smile . . . Volsky was astonished by the starkness of the choices imposed by war: if they had not succeeded in putting out the fire this mother and her child would not have survived . . . Their survival might not be of long duration, with the threat of more bombs, hunger, the plummeting of the red line in the thermometer. But this reprieve was worth the trouble of risking his life. Yes, for this woman's wan smile, for her child's calm breathing, one must forget that young man drinking his hot chocolate on a June evening and feeling proudly triumphant.

Since the start of the blockade he had never considered that saving a life at the cost of his own might become his destiny.

One November morning this close proximity of life to death permeated his very breathing. During the previous two days he had not had the strength to leave the flat. At his first attempt to go and fetch his hundred and twenty-five grams of bread he had collapsed on the stairs, spent a moment before recovering consciousness and had then taken an hour to climb back up to his room, where, thanks to the fire, his body resisted merging into the lifelessness that prevailed in the streets.

He began exploring the very last zone that precedes

extinction. He had always pictured hunger as a relent-less, gut-wrenching torment. And so it was, for as long as one had the strength to feel it. Then the torture came to an end for want of a victim, the latter having become a shadow for whom a mouthful of water already repre-sented a painful effort of digestion. The cold, too, caused suffering to those who still clung to life but deadened the pain of those who were utterly exhausted and waiting for the end. Yet this increasing weakness seemed to be external to the body. It was the world that was changing, making objects too heavy (the can in which the water was heating now weighed a ton), lengthening distances (three days before he had managed to reach the bakery: a veritable polar expedition).

Despite the physical collapse, his mind remained clear. He contemplated the possibility of no longer being alive the following day, the strangeness of confronting this notion so calmly, and even the vanity this vision of his own death would have represented, had he not really been dying.

His brain was, indeed, functioning faultlessly. And yet it was something other than thought that one evening commanded him to extricate himself from his torpid state and embark on a journey through the icy dark-ness that filled the flat. At the far end of the shadows the violin strings were trembling at the touch of a hand.

The old couple were stretched out in their bed, which had the look of a tent where the sides, blankets and jumbled-up clothes had all collapsed on top of them. No fire in the little stove, just the light of a candle that had burned low.

'My husband is dead . . . You passed out . . .' the old woman murmured and it took Volsky a moment to realize that the two remarks had not been made at the same time. He had had a brief blackout, the woman had got up to lay a scrap of moistened cloth on his face and, as he came to, he heard her voice ('You passed out . . .'). He tried to explain that it was not her telling him about the death that had thrown him to the ground, as in a bad stage play. She assured him it had not occurred to her, helped him to sit down in the armchair. They no longer had the strength to speak, their silence became a vigil in which their mutual understanding needed no words.

They understood that death had ceased to surprise, it occurred too frequently in this city *in extremis*. Many were the flats inhabited by corpses, dead bodies were deposited in the public streets, only a slender frontier separating them from the living. Volsky remembered a passer-by stopping at the entrance to Palace Bridge one day, beside a man stretched out in the snow, who suddenly collapsed himself, joining the man on the far side of that frontier. 'I almost did that just now,' he thought, glancing at the old man's body.

Death had always been cordoned off in his mind by a complex game of hide and seek with himself, in which he veered between perfumed promises, cynicism and fear. He had come across the same contrivances in books: a maze of prevarications for keeping quiet about death, if not dressing it up in lies . . .

The woman reached out her hand, adjusted the candle. The flame made her emaciated hand transparent, the pattern of the blood vessels was clear. Fingers

111

of ice. The shadow of her gesture passed over the old man's face like a caress and seemed to animate it with a trace of life. She must have noticed this, smiled as she closed her husband's eyes and squeezed his hand.

All that Volsky had known about death now seemed false. This moment he shared with these two ancient beings was vibrant with life. A life clarified in the ultimate simplicity of truth. These old hands joined, this grieving smile on the woman's face, the calm of her gaze.

Late in the night she put a little canvas bag on the bedside table and, more rapidly than his eyes, Volsky's sense of smell detected dry bread. 'We're going to be able to eat,' the woman whispered, as if she were afraid of disturbing her husband's sleep, and she added: 'Thanks to him . . .' Words whose meaning Volsky could not follow. The dry bread swelled deliciously in the mouth. And with it this taste his tongue had difficulty in recognizing, a lump of sugar that dissolved slowly, becoming not a taste but a vision, the shifting mosaic of a forgotten world. 'We shouldn't eat too much,' they both remarked automatically. The well-known refrain of all starving people facing the danger of sudden abundance. Too much . . . Volsky looked at the little bag, calculated the time his neighbour might be able to hold on with this reserve supply.

'Yes, thanks to him,' she repeated. A letter left by her husband had told her about the existence of this bag hidden behind those books that had not yet been burned in the stove. For weeks now the man had been saving a part of his ration, knowing that between himself and his wife a choice had to be made as to who should survive . . .

Volsky had already heard tell of such people in Leningrad in the siege who let themselves die to save a loved one, generally a mother sacrificing herself for her children. Now he himself owed his life to a man.

The old woman fell silent, shut her eyes, her hand clasping her husband's fingers. Volsky once more had the feeling that the bond between them was indifferent to the demise of bodies. The woman took a deep breath and, with the wry smile that was familiar to him, murmured: 'As a matter of fact, I did the same . . .' With a nod of her head towards a little set of shelves, she indicated a paper package from which she extracted slices of dried bread.

He set off for the cemetery in the dense black of a winter morning. Shadowy main thoroughfares, empty of traffic, were evocative of frozen fjords from which the sea had withdrawn. There were more passers-by than he would have expected. They stood out against the darkness, as if on a photographic negative. The ones going to the factory walked faster and looked less downcast, Volsky noticed, not knowing whether this impression of energy was due to the extra bread they received or to their robust constitutions. More frequently than these workmen, women passed by, drawing sledges laden with buckets, some empty, some filled with water from the Neva. Their gait did not differ from the shuffling of people who, like Volsky, were transporting a dead person.

113

He had used a wardrobe door, a plank a couple of feet wide, to support the old man's body. Rare were those who managed to find a coffin. Most people buried their loved ones in a shroud made from a curtain or a tablecloth.

After three or four crossroads you no longer had to turn into different streets to get to the cemetery and from now on everyone was moving in the same direction. Volsky waded through the snow a short distance behind two women whose burden had been placed on a rectangle of sheet metal. They came to a corner and stopped, one of them embraced the other before leaving her. She had helped her for part of the way and now had to go off to work, thought Volsky. The one who was left in her harness advanced more slowly now and soon he was on the point of overtaking her. It was then that he noticed his mistake. What he had taken for sheet metal was, in reality, a large painting . . . Amazing and yet not so, he told himself, picturing the disarray, the haste, the impossibility of quickly finding a sledge . . . The figure swathed in cloth and lying at the centre of the frame did not appear to be heavy, the canvas sagged very little. But to slide such a rectangle along called for strenuous efforts: the corners of the picture caught in the snow, the body slithered around, risked falling off . . .

More with a gesture than with words, Volsky offered his help, the woman accepted with a simple nod of her head. With one hand he was now pulling her load. The black of the sky turned to violet, limpid, icy. The line of the street, the white filaments of breath above the walkers, could be seen more clearly.

The sound of aircraft arose while they were crossing a large empty square. 'The worst kind,' Volsky said to himself, hearing the screams of the Stuka dive-bombers. They could feel the blast from the explosions in the soles of their feet and the din reverberated through the scenery of the dead city. A huge cloud arose from the next street, swirling around itself. The people abandoned their dead and rushed into the entrance halls to blocks of flats. Volsky and the woman he was helping found themselves lying against a wall, behind snowdrifts. She was stretched out on her side, her arms shielding her face. Without knowing anything about her, unaware of whether she was young or old, Volsky felt intense pity for this body flung down amid the dirty snow. Just one fragment of shrapnel and this unknown woman could be left there, an inert piece of human debris. He had an impulse to stand up, to interpose himself between this life and the spurts of metal riddling the street.

After a quarter of an hour they resumed their journey and Volsky could finally see the face of the woman walking beside him. She was young, but her hunger-ravaged features made her ageless, almost without personality. Like all the women in the besieged city. Eyes enlarged and sunken, emaciated cheek lines that allowed the geometry of the jaws and the skull to show through.

When they stopped, breathless, to crunch some dried bread, he spoke, wanting to lighten the weight of their funereal progress.

'I'd never have expected to be giving my neighbour a ride on a contraption like this. It's sad . . . And yours isn't much better provided for . . . Who is that?'

'It's my mother.'

They remained still, facing one another, silent, avoiding the slightest facial expression, resisting the onset of tears. It was thirty degrees below that morning, it was not the moment to weep.

The young woman came to life first, bent down, seized the rope attached to her load.

'I've changed more than you, Georgy,' she murmured. 'You don't recognize me.'

Volsky thought he had misheard, amazed by the way she addressed him but also by the speed at which this woman's voice was once more becoming familiar. Yet he was still looking at a stranger.

'Have we met before?'

The young woman slightly lifted the thick shawl that hid her forehead.

'Yes. I'm the one who doesn't know how to eat pastries and you love hot chocolate.'

He stopped, thunderstruck, stared at her emaciated features, the huge, darkly ringed eyes . . . Mila!

One evening at the beginning of December Leningrad moved beyond words. Until recently these had been of some help in thinking about its icy death throes. One could say 'war', 'blockade', 'famine' and it all seemed logical. Until the day when, at the Five Corners intersection, Volsky and Mila saw an expanse of frozen water. Pipes had burst, leaving a vast mirror filled with purple sky and dark facades. They had been proceeding one step at a time, pausing every five minutes to catch their breath. Reaching the open space they stopped, dumbfounded. An unknown city was revealed in the reflection yawning at their feet. At the edge of this abyss sat a young woman, a statue covered in hoar frost. Words contrived as best they could to reconstruct what had happened: a girl had tried to draw water there, had sat down, overcome with exhaustion. But words were shattered by this upside-down city, by the smile that could be made out on the girl's frozen face.

The previous day they had helped the old woman, Volsky's neighbour, to leave the city. This tiny chance of getting away currently existed thanks to lorries that ventured across the frozen surface of Lake Ladoga. This route was not yet referred to by the people of Leningrad as 'The Road of Life' but hundreds fled the city in this

117

way, blessing the cold that solidified the waves, the cold that was deadly for those who remained . . . This escape route was the last scrap of meaning they could cling to in the dead city. The war, the siege, these lorries carrying children and old people to survival. Words and actions still linked in a semblance of logic . . .

The dusk at Five Corners turned that world upside down onto the purple surface of the ice – a vertiginous vision of blocks of flats, street lamps, stars plunged deep into the earth. And at the edge of the frozen water, a girl seated there, smiling from the depths of her death.

They hardly spoke any more. Words had lost their grip on what they were living through. They would have had to refer to these blocks of stone harbouring corpses as 'houses'. And these vague, angular sketches of humanity as 'townspeople'. 'Food' meant boiled leather, and the paste from wallpaper diluted in water.

To protect these last sparks of life, thousands of women, thin as skeletons, worked flat out at the conveyor belts of munitions factories, lining up rows of shells, thunderous streams of bullets. On the icy plains surrounding the city, men with faces furrowed by chilblains were hurling this steel against other men, who, with insane obstinacy, sought to conquer the immense graveyard that Leningrad was turning into. Every night the lorries set out across the ice of the lake, exposed targets that had to pit their wits against the bombers hounding them in the midst of the snow. Often the human cargo would vanish through the holes opened up by the bombs. On their return journey the lorries that got through brought bread, from which one-hundred-and-twenty-five-gram slices could be cut, giving a new lease, for a few more days, to this life words could no longer describe.

And above this ghostly world the mauve sun of the great frosts would rise, a dull disc, making only a brief appearance, inspiring thoughts of some unknown planet.

Everything that happened to them seemed as if it were taking place following their death. In an afterlife where, deep in labyrinths of stone, unique beings were dying, lost amid the confusion of emaciated bodies, amid the frenzy of the last shudders of hope, amid the fever of memories, while other human beings, a little more robust, were cutting out pieces of metal which men with faces scorched by the cold employed to kill those who had come to these snowy wastes to die.

This was how Volsky and Mila now saw the world, from a very remote perspective. A perspective that could have seemed godlike in its detachment yet was grievously human, for each of them greatly dreaded the other's death.

On that evening when they saw the city turned upside down, this dread had eyes that spied on them in the darkness. They had come home, had tried to light the fire, had failed. Their hands, made clumsy from weakness, could no longer manage to break up a piece of flooring. Someone was staring at them in the darkness with a scornful grimace, like a hunter contemplating his prey as it quakes at his feet . . .

Volsky turned away from this gaze, seized a bundle of sheets of paper, crumpled them one by one, filled the stove with them. All the books had already been burned, all that was left was these pages of sheet music and an opera libretto they had once been studying at the Conservatoire. The fire was lit, they held out their hands to it, massaged their fingers, managed to dislodge a dozen or so blocks of wood.

As the sheets blazed, ripples of music and singing went up in smoke. Fear yielded to an unknown feeling: perhaps death was the birth of these echoes escaping from the burnt pages. This certainty of being some-where other than in their starving bodies had nothing triumphant about it. Quite simply, without needing to say it, they knew this is how it was.

The next day this faith gave them the strength to go to the place where they had met on 21 June . . . The Nord Café was shut, the street closed off with blocks of concrete, the entrances to the buildings transformed into machine-gun posts. The city was preparing to undergo the final assault from the enemy. The inside of the café had changed little. The same counter with its bronze top, the same mirrors, and there, beneath a big mosaic on the wall, 'their' table . . . Yes, a table in an empty room, bathed in coppery sunlight, deep calm. And in the window pane the reflection of two faces with their bones protruding from their skulls. So this was what death was.

They knew they were too far away from their building

and that the crust of bread eaten that morning would not be enough for the return journey. The streets were lined with frozen bodies, some of them wrapped in makeshift shrouds, others sitting or lying there, frozen in the pose determined by their collapse. They walked slowly, experiencing no emotion at the sight of these dead people, nor at the idea, hazy and painless, of falling, becoming rigid. At one point Volsky noticed that Mila's chin had turned white, it looked like a smear of powder, the warning sign of frostbite. He tried to rub this spot but he could barely command his numb fingers. Then he opened his coat for the young woman to lay her frozen face against his chest. They remained there, hugging one another in the middle of a street where, in the dusk, the dead kept watch. It was their first embrace.

Turning towards the Neva they saw a long queue outside a building. Famished as they were, they instinctively made the link: a crowd, ration tickets, a piece of bread. But this queue had an unusual look about it. People were going in at the door but no one was coming out, as if they had decided to eat their rations on the spot, away from the icy blast coming off the Baltic Sea. As they drew closer Volsky and Mila discovered to their amazement that this was a theatre and people, rendered mute with exhaustion, were going to watch a performance. The poster for the Musical Comedy Theatre announced an operetta: *The Three Musketeers* . . .

Without conferring, they moved towards the stage door. An old man, candle in hand, reminiscent of a lost character in a Chekhov play, greeted them, led them to the manager's office. The latter was in the middle of breaking up wood and stoking an iron stove on which a saucepan was warming. He raised an emaciated face to them and his smile stretched the skin on his angular cheekbones. His eyes seemed fixed on a vision of horror. Volsky mentioned the Conservatoire, asked if they could be useful . . .

Suddenly the man thrust him aside and, by moving adroitly, just had time to catch Mila as she passed out. When she came to he murmured, still with that smile which left the expression in his eyes unaltered: 'In the old days actors were trained to support heroines who fainted . . .' He invited them to drink a bowl of soup, which was, in fact, hot water with a little meal floating in it.

Their offer was accepted with a remark Volsky would remember for the rest of his life: 'We need voices.' His eyes met Mila's. Voices . . . In truth, that was all they had left.

Their lives merged with that of the theatre. They assisted in putting up scenery, gave a helping hand to wardrobe, cooked meals for the singers and musicians. And in the evening they went on stage. Volsky believed that by engaging an excess of walk-on actors, the director was seeking to encourage them. But after several perform-ances he realized that this casting related to the frequency with which the actors died. By taking part in the show, the walk-ons were learning all the roles and could thus take over from anyone who, one day, did not return.

Volsky and Mila already knew this *Three Musketeers* by heart, an operetta written by a certain Louis Varney, the libretto of which had been substantially reworked by a Russian author. The piece had very little in common with the novel by Dumas. Apart from the musketeers, of course. When they got home they lit the fire, rehearsed the songs and on occasion burst out laughing, as the line about 'the hot southern sun' caused a cloud of mist to emerge from Volsky's mouth . . . The hardest part was in the first act, when thanks to this 'hot southern sun' Marie, d'Artagnan's beloved, had to stand there shivering in a pale satin dress.

Everyone strove for the performances to go on as before. But, of course, everything was very different.

They acted by candlelight in an auditorium where it was ten degrees below. Often the show was interrupted by an air-raid siren. The audience would go down into the basement, those who no longer had the strength to do so remaining huddled in their seats, staring at the stage emptied by the sound of bombing . . . Applause was no longer heard. Too weak, their hands frozen in mittens, people would bow to thank the actors. This silent gratitude was more touching than any number of ovations.

One evening, just before the performance, one of the musketeers stumbled on the threshold of his dressing room and collapsed, with a surprised smile still on his made-up face . . . It was not the first death Volsky and Mila had witnessed here at the theatre, but this time they were the ones who carried the actor to the cemetery. The road was familiar and along the way the real difference between the performances now staged and the life of the theatre before the war was brought home to them. Death was something those singing on stage shared with those listening in the auditorium. A theatrical illusion created so close to extinction acquired the force of a supreme truth.

This truth was even more alive in the concerts the singers gave at the front. Frozen plains, ploughed up by shells, makeshift platforms balanced on ammunition boxes and the faces of soldiers, most of whom would die during the days ahead. Volsky and Mila often found themselves singing songs from *The Three Musketeers*, this was their 'dress rehearsal', they would say with a smile.

They would not have believed that the front line was so close to Leningrad. When they mounted the platform they could see the frozen oscillogram of spires and domes through the cold grey mist. Their voices seemed to soar up like a fragile screen between this city and the enemy positions. They met the looks of the soldiers, young or older men, some maintaining a certain bold front, others drained, devoid of hope. The songs spoke of sunshine and love. But what could be glimpsed at times in these looks was the terrible brotherhood of the doomed. Yes, the acceptance of death, but also the mad certainty of being more than this body hurled beneath the bombs.

The singers were easy prey now for the machine-gun fire from dive-bombing aircraft. And yet it was here, at the front, sharing a meal with the fighting men, that Volsky and Mila regained a little strength. One evening at the theatre Volsky remarked: 'Thanks to their mess cooking, I could play d'Artagnan now from start to finish . . .' In the early days, they recalled, they had had to sit down and catch their breath at the end of each scene.

When Volsky spoke of playing d'Artagnan he was joking, never imagining that one day he could be given a part, albeit a supporting one. However, the allocation of roles was no longer decided by the director but by a silent being, present at every performance. The grim reaper himself, whom the actors used to make the butt of their mockery, to keep their courage up.

*   *   *

125

The singer who played Marie was fatally wounded in a bombing raid a few yards away from the theatre. Mila had to take over from her that same evening. During the interval, while roguish tunes still hung on the air, she ran to the dressing room where the actress, surrounded by singers and musicians, was dying. When she saw Mila, she whispered: 'In the second act, when you're escaping with d'Artagnan, don't move too fast. Otherwise you'll be out of breath from running. The first few times, I remember . . .' Her voice broke off, her eyes fastened on a tall candle flame. The bell announced the start of the next act.

Two days later, Volsky played d'Artagnan. He took over from an actor who had been found lifeless in a flat with shattered windows.

The show went ahead without mistakes. There were not even any air-raid warnings to interrupt it. Only Volsky knew that his performance was hanging by a thread. Halfway through the play his strength deserted him. He did not collapse however, and continued to brandish his sword and sing lustily. But a split perception took over: his body trudged up the steps to a castle, his voice pealed out in merry runs, while far away from this performance the words of someone at several years' distance threw out their echo. In the icy darkness of the auditorium, he could see the spectators bowing, apologetic about no longer being able to clap. And on stage a young woman was singing to whom he had just declared his love, following the play's storyline. He sensed that for her their theatrical kiss had been more than a piece of stage business required by the plot. This detail should have amused him, yet he felt an intense sadness that seemed to come from a future in which their stage embrace would have quite a different meaning . . . He also noticed that the actor playing Porthos was sweating profusely.

Instead of putting him off, this split perception enabled him to carry on right up to the moment when, holding hands, the actors walked forward to greet the audience. Mila was smiling, moved, her face on fire; Porthos was bowing, breathless, brushing the boards with his musketeer's hat; Volsky could feel the song he had just been singing still throbbing in his throat. It was even possible to imagine the swell of applause and the beautiful bare shoulders of the women in the audience . . .

His joy then found a selfish rationale, a hunger for admiration which reminded him of that young man drinking his hot chocolate: a summery past that would surely be reborn; life, his young life would resume its course, the nightmare of a starving Leningrad would pass, and the city would not fall!

He went into his dressing room, tossed his plumed hat into an armchair, removed the shoulder belt and sword, peeled away the moustache, wincing into the mirror. And suddenly, in the same reflection, caught sight of Porthos. The man was sitting in a corner, like a punished child, his hands clasped between his knees, his face shining with sweat. Volsky was about to go and clap him on the shoulder, to congratulate him on his performance when Mila appeared and beckoned to him to come away . . . The previous night Porthos had managed to get his wife and children onto one of those lorries that evacuated the rare lucky ones out of the besieged city. That morning he had learned that the convoy had been bombed and there were no survivors. He had come to the theatre, given a performance. The stage was poorly lit, the audience did not see his tears. Even the cast thought he had a fever and was perspiring in spite of the cold.

They went home in silence, walking along the dark streets where one often came across frozen bodies. In the sky, mingling with the snowflakes, there fluttered sheets of paper which the passers-by picked up, read, destroyed. Leaflets dropped by a German aircraft: Moscow had been captured, the army of the Reich had crossed the Volga and was advancing into the Urals, meeting no resistance . . . It was vitally important not to be tempted to believe this for a second, danger lay in doubt taking root in the mind, undermining all resolve.

No, Moscow could not surrender! They thought about Leningrad, remembered the mud-caked faces of the soldiers hanging on to a narrow strip of frozen plain a few miles from there.

'Those lorries that were bombed in the night,' murmured Mila. 'I was told about it just before the show. I didn't think he'd be able to hold on to the end . . .' She stooped and picked up several leaflets, 'for the fire,' she said with a little smile. They walked on. That man in tears who had sung and laughed on stage became a fragile but strangely irrefutable proof for them: no, the city would not fall.

*　　*　　*

The next day they learned that further performances were going to be suspended, the mobilization of the remaining men who were not yet at the front had just been decreed.

And in the evening, walking along the embankments beside the Neva, they saw sailors carrying big black crates and loading them onto a tug. Volsky tried to get close, a soldier sent him packing. They did an about-turn and walked back beside an old man who, like them, must have seen the loading of the cargo. 'I was in the navy myself,' he explained softly. 'What they're doing is mining the harbour. Then they'll sink all the warships. So as to leave nothing for the Germans. It's finished. Our city's lost.'

For several days they gave concerts close to the front line, where death could occur between a couple of remarks exchanged in a trench. The same wind, at thirty below, which seemed to sheathe their singing in a layer of ice, the same shivering which the actors concealed behind bold gestures. But the looks they encountered in the crowd of soldiers had changed. These men now knew that their deaths could protect no one. To save Moscow, where the resistance was already being broken by the Germans, Leningrad was to be sacrificed. That winter the old rivalry between the two capitals posed an impossible choice.

The singers no longer returned home, they were billeted in a workers' hostel emptied by the mobilization. From this outlying area it was easier to get to the front. Several times already they had asked to be armed, so they could be sent to a fighting unit. But, curiously enough, the old soldier who used to escort their troupe would always echo the reply given that day by the manager of the Musical Comedy Theatre: 'We need your voices . . .'

He said it again one evening, when he told them that the following day their concert would take place at a very exposed site. 'You will be singing under fire,' he added. 'So only volunteers are to come with me.' The response was a torrent of cheerfully indignant exclamations. 'Oh Captain, do you doubt your musketeers?' one of the actors burst out, the song sung by Porthos. The 'captain' hushed them with a gesture. 'That's all I can tell you. The conditions will be really tough. Think about it . . .'

They set off just before dawn in an army truck: fourteen singers, ten musicians carrying their instruments, no one refused the call. The journey was short (there were no long distances around the besieged city any more) and the spot where they piled out did not look very different from the places where their concerts generally took place. Except that this time no human presence was visible. The gleaming pinpricks of stars, a white expanse sloping down to a frozen river, then rising up to a ridge above the opposite bank. No sound apart from their whispers (the 'captain' had asked them not to speak out loud). No platform, they took up position on a square of packed snow, the singers in front, the musicians a little way behind them, all facing the river, more in response to an instinct than to any order. Over there beyond the ridge, a mysterious listening presence could be sensed . . .

Their military guide passed among them, shook each one's hand, sometimes muttering a proverb ('No one dies twice, no one escapes a single death'), sometimes wishing them good luck in words which sounded bizarre coming from an army officer: 'Off you go now, with

God's help.' His tones were muffled but the emotion sincere and that was the moment when they realized this would be a concert quite unlike the previous ones.

'Look, that's the star you can see from my window . . .' Volsky had time to murmur in Mila's ear. She had time to look up . . .

The plain, which had looked bare, shivered into life and was covered in tiny dots. The night, caught off guard, remained silent for several seconds, then suddenly erupted into gunfire. The dull sound of a 'hurrah!' swelled in the air. The 'captain' waved his arm, the music rang out. With the power of their voices the singers drowned the shouting of the soldiers and the first shots.

They sang the 'Internationale', hardly surprised at the 'captain's' choice (their usual repertoire was more lyrical). There were few fervent believers in communism among them, but the words bursting forth from their lips spoke of a truth it was difficult to deny. One appearing right before their eyes. To begin with the white plain bristling with little black figures running down towards the river. Then the first bodies falling and on the ridge above the opposite bank the German positions revealing themselves, breaking the line of snowy dunes with indentations made for their machine-guns. Finally, in the glorious clear light of this winter morning, a long scarlet stain left by a soldier crawling back towards the singers, as if they could have protected him.

All was confusion on both banks. A wave of attackers fell back, decimated, and collided with the next line as it moved into the assault, joined with it, managed to advance several dozen yards, fell beneath the increasingly accurate fire from the Germans. Yet another dotted line of human beings rose up and hurled itself at the icy slope on the far shore. The crackling of the gunfire became continuous, rhythmed by explosions, the shouts of the commanding officers and the cries of the wounded. In particular those of that wounded man still crawling up towards the musicians, emitting a harrowing death rattle and spattering the snow with his blood.

To the anarchy of all these deaths the singing gave a solemn, measured rhythm, which seemed to resonate beyond the battlefield. They were few in number on their stage of compacted snow, but it felt to the soldiers as if the power of the whole country rose behind them.

They were embarking on the anthem for the third time when Volsky noticed the fighting men who had reached the top of the bank opposite. A burst of machine-gun fire mowed them down, but their bodies marked the most advanced frontier of the assault. He could see it all, despite the effort the singing demanded. On the frozen river, men were grappling with a gun-carriage, its wheels embedded in a snowdrift. Their movements were both frenzied and painfully slow, like those of someone running in a nightmare.

He also saw what the darkness had hidden: at the bottom of the valley a ruined village, charred roofs and, amazingly intact, one house beneath a very tall tree, miraculously preserved. The quirk of a day of warfare . . . Another quirk, that young wounded

133

soldier, huddled close to the singers, gazing at them in tears. The logical suffering of that mass of human beings and suddenly this singular suffering, which no logic could justify.

The assault was an act of desperate bravery, a heroic last stand rather than a strategists' decision. Long years after the war Volsky would come across references to that day in December in two history books. The first would speak of 'the participation of the artists of Leningrad in the defence of the city', without referring to anyone in particular. The second, much more recent, would refer to 'a sham counter-offensive dreamed up by those responsible, seeking to clear their names in Stalin's eyes'. Neither one nor the other would make any mention of the soldier who had just traced a line of blood in the snow, of the tranquillity of that house, safe beneath its tree, or, least of all, of the lock of dark hair that had escaped from under Mila's headscarf, and was stirred by Volsky's breath as he sang.

No history, either, would record that line of soldiers who managed to haul themselves up onto the ridge. Their silhouettes were etched against the sky before being felled by bullets, the following wave managed to cling on a little further up. The singers lost count of the number of times they had struck up the 'Internationale', but, at the sight of these men, as the words about 'the final conflict' rang out, they were freshly apposite.

It was then that the explosions began to occur all around them. Later on, in the army, Volsky would learn to recognize this as mortar fire, with its perfidious trajectories straight up into the air, which create the impression that the shells are falling out of the sky. All he noticed at the time was the increasing accuracy of the fire closing in on them. An explosion threw up snow behind the band and, without turning round, he sensed from a jolt in the music that one of the musicians had been hit. The singers reinforced their voices with wild exhilaration, glad to be identified by the enemy and therefore counting for something in this fight.

He fell without being wounded. A singer on his right who had caught a shell splinter full in the face, toppled backwards and brought him down. In the time it took to get up Volsky saw their troupe as they must appear from the water's edge: two rows of singers, a semicircle of musicians and gaps already left by those who had been killed. Yet the singing had lost none of its intensity. And on the ridge several dozen soldiers were fighting on, hurling grenades, setting up machine-guns among the bodies of their dead comrades.

They should have fallen back, retreated, escaped to the truck. Saved themselves. No one stirred. The order to fall back could have been given but their 'captain' now lay on the path leading down to the river . . . They sang with a freedom never before experienced. Scorn for death caused a fierce exultation to well up in their emaciated bodies. Tears shone upon their eyelashes. Volsky saw one of the singers, his head all bloody, trying to rise to his feet and return to his place. Then a cymbal went rolling down the icy slope.

And now silence swept in, the light turned into a

darkness from out of which emerged words he was struggling to make sense of. So it was . . . The effort he made woke him up. In the cotton-wool density left by an explosion he could hear a voice and when his sight returned he found himself lying among other bodies and very close to his face he saw Mila's eyes, her dark brown locks, no longer covered by her shawl and, high up on her brow, a long wound. He spoke but could not hear himself. The only audible words were those she was crooning softly. Lines sung by Marie, from the operetta they had been performing in . . .

Before losing consciousness again he stared at this woman's face bent over him, a face furrowed by hunger and disfigured by wounds. And, very briefly, he experienced the start of a life he would never have thought possible on this earth.

He did not see Mila again, did not even know if she had been treated in Leningrad or perhaps evacuated one night in a convoy of lorries. Discharged from hospital on New Year's Eve, he found himself in an artillery battery a few miles from the spot where their last concert had taken place. The stranglehold of the blockade had loosened a little, it had been possible to retake a few small towns from the enemy and in one of them Volsky's comrades picked up a packet of elegant cards with a German text printed in fine gothic lettering. An officer read them, spat out an oath. They were invitations to the celebration to mark the fall of Leningrad. The festivities were planned for 18 December at the Astoria Hotel. Volsky remembered that their choir had been singing two days before that date.

He felt proud to have assisted, through this concert, in the defence of the city. Before learning that in mid-December the Germans had been defeated close to Moscow, and that this had saved Leningrad, making those fine invitation cards, with their gothic script, surplus to requirements . . . Impossible in war to judge between the impact of collective action and that of individual heroism, the fluctuating imprecision of weighing both in the balance – this would be one of the lessons of those four years of fighting.

The war had little else to teach him. In the siege of Leningrad he had lived with death as intimately as a soldier would have done. Now, crossing fields strewn with corpses, he was astonished at their number, but the absolute singularity of each death was somewhat blunted here at the front, blurred by this very number.

Of course, there was a mass of detail, often of vital importance, for him to learn. That unharmed house in a village razed to the ground and the very tall tree he had seen during their last concert. He knew now that it was the tree which had protected the shack. A target that, logically, should have been the first to be blown up. But gunners have their own logic. They take aim by selecting a reference point (a church tower, a post or a tree) and it is the reference point that survives amid the ruins, as a reward for its value in pinpointing targets.

He also had a memory of those soldiers shuffling about beside their gun on the riverbank on the day of the desperate attack. From now on his war was just this shuffling about, in snow or mud, and he came no longer to expect glorious feats of arms, dazzling exploits. Resigned himself to studying the crude mechanics of battle. Soon he could evaluate at a glance the steel of the armoured vehicles he was aiming at. His ear could judge the calibre of guns being fired, the different whistlings of the shells. Distances, trajectories took on a palpable density, inscribed in the very air he breathed.

And then, on occasion, all this knowledge became

138

futile, as on a particular evening at the end of an engagement. The shooting had stopped, his comrades were rolling their cigarettes and suddenly one of them fell over, with a little red mark above his temple: a stray fragment of shrapnel. No glorious goal would compensate for this young face frozen, this unique presence, turning into dead matter before their eyes. Yes, he learned this lesson as well: in war the most testing moments are those of peace, for a dead man lying in the grass makes the living see the world as it would be, but for their folly. It was a spring day, the battle had taken place near a forest where the undergrowth was white with wild cherry trees in flower and lilies of the valley.

He was posted to the front defending Leningrad. Then transferred to the Volga, to a city that must at all costs be victorious for it bore Stalin's name. In this battle a bullet grazed his face, his left cheek was gashed, leaving a scar like a little grin. 'You're never sad with me,' he took to joking.

A year later, in the gigantic battle of Kursk, Volsky became unrecognizable.

He had already seen what hell one day, a beautiful spring day, of warfare could be. But previously these had been hells controlled by men. This time the creators lost control of their own handiwork. Instead of an offensive in which the infantry made the running, with the artillery in support, it was a monstrous confrontation between thousands of tanks, hordes of black tortoises, their carapaces ramming one another, spitting fire, ejecting human beings from their blazing shells who burned like torches. The sky was filled with smoke, the air reeked of exhaust from the engines. No sound could be heard above the explosions and the grinding of over-heated metal. With his fellow gunners, Volsky found himself hemmed in against the remains of a fortified post, unable either to retreat or properly to open fire. The duels between tanks were happening too close at hand, too fast, the gun would have had to be handled with the dexterity of a revolver. Nevertheless they tried their luck, hit the turret of a Tiger, but glancingly, and received a burst of machine-gun fire in reply. A heavy black tortoise had just located them. Keeping his eyes fixed on the manoeuvrings of the monster, Volsky signalled to those behind him to bring up the shell. No one stirred. He turned: one gunner was dead, another sat there, his face streaming with red, his screams muted by the noise.

What followed had the slowness of a nightmare, so familiar to him, in which each action seemed to take long minutes. A shell to be lifted out of the crate, the sleek heaviness of a toy asleep in his hands, to be carried, inserted into the breech, loaded, then he began to take aim . . . Interminable seconds during which the tank lowered its gun towards him, as if the man aiming it were amusing himself by taking his time. No hell could be such a torment.

What happened next would be pieced together later,

at nightfall, when he became capable of remembering, of understanding. He had no time to fire and yet the turret of the Tiger blew up, flinging out the bodies crammed together in its cockpit. The violence of the explosion threw Volsky to the ground and momentarily he glimpsed the angular carapace of another monster, the enormous self-propelling gun, the famous SU-152, that killer of tanks, which had just saved his life . . .

The evening spilled down sluggish rain. Having recovered the use of his ears he could hear the hissing of the water on the incandescent metal of the armoured vehicles. Groans across the plain encumbered with black machines. Words spoken in Russian, allowing him to understand whose the victory was in this clash of steel.

And suddenly, appearing in the half light, this teetering silhouette: a German from a tank unit, stunned, no doubt, wandering blindly among the carapaces. Volsky drew his gun, aimed . . . But did not fire. The soldier was young and seemed indifferent to what could happen to him after the horror of what he had just lived through. Their eyes met and, in spite of themselves, they waved a hand at one another. Volsky put away his pistol, the soldier disappeared into the summer dusk.

The night was brief and by about three a.m. an ashen pallor was already casting a glow over the surrounding area. He got up, climbed onto a low wall in the fortified post. The mist lifted over the plain to the hazy limits of the horizon. And its whole surface was hidden under the dark armature of tangled tanks. A human presence could be sensed within all this metallic darkness:

wounded men, Russian or German, waiting in the suffo-cating heat of the turrets. Men burned, with wounds beyond hope, whose eyes could see the sky which the rain had now left and a star poised directly above . . . He thought . . . 'above this hell,' but the word seemed imprecise. Hell teemed with little torturers, eager to inflict suffering on the fallen. Here the wounded awaited death in the solitude of a block of steel, pressed up against the bodies of dead comrades.

He caught himself making no distinction between the Russian and the German wounded. The hell created by men . . . Disturbed by a truth that was taking hold of him, he hastened to return to a more clear-cut judgement: the enemy had just been beaten and these Germans dying in their tanks had deserved it . . . Yet that perception of the suffering of all mankind was not easy to eradicate. In it Volsky sensed a great and terrible wisdom which bowed him down beneath the weight of a very old man's experience. In the siege of Leningrad he had already come to see human lives as one single communal life and it was perhaps this perception that gave him hope.

Before the sun rose he heard a bird calling, briefly, repeatedly, with rather muted resonance. A dull, humble song, but one which rang out for all the living and the dead.

The soldier who helped Volsky to carry his comrades' bodies greeted him oddly: 'Now then, chin up, Grandad!' Grandad! Volsky smiled, telling himself that, drained by a sleepless night, the other man, the same age as himself, was babbling nonsense. He would have thought no more about that incongruous greeting but then the nurse, who was putting a dressing on his wrist, concluded: 'There you are, Grandpa. Like that you'll be all set for the next battle.' He burst out laughing and saw a flicker of doubt in the woman's eyes. A mirror hung on the wall of the dressing station. He went up to it . . . And clapped his hand to his head, as if to hide it. His hair was white, that snowy white which some old men sport with such elegance.

From that day onwards he stopped writing to Mila. The blockade of Leningrad continued and Volsky knew what that signified for a woman who had already been living through it for two years. He could imagine the city under siege in summer, those thousands of buildings filled with corpses . . . No letter from Mila had reached him: the postal service rarely broke through the mesh of the blockade. Besides how could he be found, with his transfers from one front to another? Dreaming up all these reasons helped him to think that Mila was still alive.

On the day after the Battle of Kursk, when he saw himself in the mirror at the dressing station, all these speculations about the mail became pointless. This old soldier with a strangely young face, scarred with a slight rictus, was another man.

This other man went back to the war almost serenely, telling himself that the person he had once been no longer existed, a little as if he had been killed. The extinguishing of all hope made a good soldier of him. No letters, no waiting for letters, no becoming emotional, which, in war, is the frequent cause of carelessness and hence of death. He became fused with the gun he served, became effectively mechanical, impassive, thrifty with words. And as time passed he even ceased to be surprised when young people addressed him as 'Grandpa'.

He had also changed in what he had once considered to be his true nature, his dream, his gift: singing. Sometimes he would sing along in chorus with his comrades, during a halt, or as he marched in a column of men cheating their weariness with merry tunes. These songs pleased him, evocative as they were of the immediate reality of the war. The banality of death, the carefree spirit of a summer's day, the scent of grass at the edge of a forest, a handful of berries swiftly gathered among the trees, and pausing there, as he glanced at the column of soldiers, a thought that made him feel giddy: 'I'm no longer among them, I'm in this forest, there are these flowers, the drowsy buzzing of bees . . .' Then he would run back to take his place among the men, singing as they marched towards death.

The speed at which their faces, lit up by singing, were obliterated in the daily slaughter, the ease with which a human being could be wiped out, was the only reality that never ceased to trouble Volsky. And it was thanks to their communal singing that he kept a memory of the faces of so many men who were gone. With his professional's ear, albeit battered by gunfire, he could recall their voices (fine, dull, touching

144

in their enthusiasm or naively reckless) and this pattern of sounds would bring a look or a smile back to life. These lives, swept away by the war, survived through song.

Thus he came to dislike those grand operatic arias he had dreamed of in the old days. All those stentorian Boris Godunovs, thrusting out their beards the better to squeeze out the vibrations of their vocal power at the height of tragic ecstasy, now struck him as false. Ludicrous, too, those plump legionaries in Italian opera, tinkling the scales of their brass armour. Or the ones in tailcoats, sticking out their chests like fighting cocks.

His passion for the magic of theatre was still alive. But after what he had lived through in Leningrad and later in the Battle of Kursk, he often asked himself about the purpose of such operatic spectacles. To please? To move? To distract? To titillate the ears of women with bare shoulders and men in patent-leather shoes, couples who, after the opera, would end up at a restaurant, discussing the performance of a legionary or a cockerel in tails?

Sometimes, between battles, sitting with his back against the carriage of his gun, he would start humming on his own, a murmur nobody else heard. These were generally d'Artagnan's songs.

The end of the war found him close to Berlin on the shores of a pond torn up by tank tracks. With two other soldiers he was engaged in positioning the guns

145

when the news of the victory reached them. He stood up and saw what he had already seen the day of his last concert, near Leningrad: a riverbank, soldiers clinging to a gun, survival dependent on the speed of shooting. The circle is complete, he thought, smiling at the soldiers as they yelled in delight. 'It's all over, Grandpa! Let's have a quick drink now and head for home!'

He told himself that his white hair was simply an ironic token of the interminable duration of the years spent at war. Human stories were so swiftly wiped out in death, so many cities had swept by, that his feeling of having aged quickly was not all that fanciful. A circle completed and, within it, the span of a whole life. His life.

During the first days of peace he sometimes thought of Mila, picturing how she might have felt on meeting this young man with white hair. Their past seemed to belong to a remote youth, lived through by someone else. By that person who had once, on stage, in the costume of a musketeer, kissed a young heroine freshly emerged from a convent. He told himself that the only tie that bound them was the ancient libretto of an old-fashioned operetta written by a forgotten author.

'To you, my beloved, I shall confide my dream . . .' he sang softly on the train carrying him back to Russia. His travelling companions took him for an old soldier in a cheerful mood.

In travelling to his native village, south of Smolensk, he had no hope of discovering a past where he could start a new life. This part of Russia had first been devastated by the Red Army as they retreated, unwilling to leave anything for the enemy, then by aerial bombardment, and finally by the Germans as they withdrew, setting fire to everything that had survived the bombing. Of his own street (a row of charred *izbas*) all that was left was an old church tower, 'saved by a miracle', one old woman told him, as he questioned her about the fate of the villagers, of his own parents. A miracle . . . He did not go to the trouble of explaining that the church tower was a good reference point left intact by those who had targeted the nearby railway junction. Survivors needed to believe in miracles. There was one, as it happened, in the garden of his ruined home: a cherry tree broken in two, but whose branches had taken root again, dusted with tiny snow-white flowers.

In Leningrad the room he had once rented was occupied. His new landlady announced: 'With you, I don't have a problem. Not like one of those empty-headed young men. I only take people of a certain age . . .'

Volsky was amazed to see that, after so many had died, the flats were crammed, then realized that people were coming in from the surrounding villages, razed to the ground by the fighting. 'So the war didn't do you much harm in the end,' the woman went on. 'And now with all your medals, you'll be a grand sight.' Volsky shrugged his shoulders: what could he reply to that? So as not to seem rude, he stammered: 'Well I don't have many medals. In the artillery you're always behind the others . . .' He felt this was a stupid remark, talking about the war was not easy. What else was there that could be spoken of? The tanks with their overheated steel that made a hissing sound in the rain? The turrets where wounded men, Russian and German, were dying? Explain how his greatest joy at the front was not those little discs of medals but a fistful of wild strawberries picked in a hurry before rejoining the column of soldiers? And that his greatest fear had lasted for a few seconds at most: when the gun on a tank took aim at him, as if relishing the pleasure of terrifying him? And that those seconds had turned him into this young old man, so respectable in the eyes of a landlady? No, such things, true as they were, were impossible to admit to.

Volsky remembered feeling tongue-tied like this before: with Mila in the besieged city.

He went to see the place where she used to live. The building was still standing but a freakish bombing raid had destroyed the staircase between the ground floor and the first floor. People were getting into their homes by means of ladders. Nobody knew Mila. They were mainly provincials who had come in from their ruined villages.

Thanks to them, the city seemed rejuvenated. The people of Leningrad, who had endured the blockade, threaded their way, pale and silent, through this ill-assorted crowd. The variety of female faces was intoxicating. People spoke to one another more readily; people smiled more, everyone was eager to come to life again in an encounter, in an exchange of looks. Volsky had never engaged so much in conversations with strangers, with women. One day he spoke to two female students he encountered at the Nord Café . . . Everything was surprising about this agreeable chatter: the room, which had not changed, these laughing girls, the ease with which he touched on the war, showing off, telling how shells would occasionally hit a flight of ducks and then – what feasting! 'You have such a young voice . . .' one of them said and he caught her glancing at his white hair.

The next day he went to a hairdresser's. Offered a choice of six colours, he opted for black. While the white was giving way to darker locks he thought of Mila. 'She must be dead,' he said to himself with the brutality the war had taught him. And he sensed that this idea was killing someone within him. 'No, why dead? She's married and may well be living very close by. Besides, what ties are there between us now? We once kissed one another in an operetta. "To you, my beloved . . ." With my white hair she'd never have recognized me. But now, with this Moor's head!' He managed to recover the merry mood that had animated him the day before in the company of the two students.

*   *   *

One Saturday he went to the Kirov Opera. Before climbing up to take his seat in the balcony he studied himself furtively in the mirrors. His hair, a little too glossy, nevertheless did not look dyed. He just felt something like the stiffness of a wig at the top of his forehead. Otherwise, a young man, proud of the impact of the heavy red star fastened above his heart.

In the auditorium there were many uniforms, armour-plated with decorations, well-cut outfits hard to picture on the muddy roads of the war. 'Theatrical costumes . . .' thought Volsky, amazed at the sharpness of the comparison. Officers' stripes, gleaming boots reflecting the glitter of the great chandelier, weighty, complacent looks . . . The looks of conquerors, Volsky said to himself and, inexplicably, he felt excluded from this camp. The whiteness of the skin revealed by the women's dresses struck him like a flesh tint long forgotten . . .

The opera itself (it was *Rigoletto*) soon banished both his fake brunet's nervousness and the impact of those uniforms. He sensed something strange resonating within him, a combination of his vocal cords and his memory. He listened as a singer listens. And at one moment he felt he was breathing along with the King.

His concentration was such that when this regret reverberated in his thoughts – 'That could have been me . . .' – he gave a start, convinced that the remark had come from one of his neighbours. The applause brought him out of his reverie. He clapped like the others but his hands seemed as false to him as his dark hair.

His concentration lapsed. He now saw what many other members of the audience could see without admitting it: actors dressed up, one as a king, another as a victim of this king's lust, characters singing arias now sad, now jaunty. All this was being watched by men feeling cramped in their uniforms and women suffering, no doubt, from tight shoes put on for the occasion. And by an idiot who had dyed his hair in the hope of pleasing these women . . . Volsky smiled at this sequence of ideas and it made him forget the unease of those words: 'That could have been me . . .'

At one moment the King sang: 'I am a student . . . and poor!' He had just donned a disguise the better to seduce the heroine. He was an actor of mature years, a portly figure, whose plump face was plastered with pink make-up. There was an ambiguous voluptuousness about his fleshy thighs clad in fine knitted tights. A poor student! Volsky lowered his head to hide his smile, rubbed his chin, coughed . . . But the laughter was already bubbling up in his lungs, rising towards his throat. There were hisses of 'Sh!', he covered his face, dug his nails into his cheeks, helpless to control this explosion of mirth, and struggled towards the exit, stepping on toes, bumping into knees, pursued by enraged glances . . . The applause welled up, as if to salute the departure of this boor.

In the cool of the cloakroom area his laughter abated. A female attendant looked at him with compassion: his eyes were now red with tears. Amid his guffaws there was also sadness. A fifty-year-old with fat thighs trying to pass himself off as a student . . . That is how his comrades in the regiment would doubtless have viewed this scene, the soldiers who sang as they marched towards death.

He was on the point of leaving the theatre when the noise of the applause grew louder (someone had half opened a door). Volsky pictured the rows of splendid uniforms and evening dresses, the vigour of those hands clapping energetically. A recollection of the performances during the blockade stabbed at his memory: a theatre lit by a few candles, the appalling cold and those human shadows, lacking the strength to clap, who used to bow their thanks to the actors . . . He remained motionless, his eyes closed, but open, in truth, onto that past, the heartrending beauty of which he now appreciated.

In this reflection on days gone by a forgotten address occurred to him: the workers' hostel where their troupe had lodged to be close to the soldiers to whom they sang songs about 'the hot southern sun'.

The road leading to that outlying area took him back in time. The city centre had already wiped away many scars. But the further one travelled from the Nevsky Prospekt, the more the imprint of war was perceptible. He even saw a German tank, its tracks shattered, its gun pointing at the passing cars.

The hostel building seemed freshened up thanks to the laundry hanging at the windows. The rooms had been occupied, Volsky guessed, by the tide of *kolkhozniks* escaping from ruined villages.

He sought someone who could give him information. But without much hope: why would Mila have remained here amid all these new arrivals? A woman with blonde hair was sitting on a bench; Volsky wanted to speak to her but her posture was like that of one asleep, her chin resting on her chest, her hands relaxed . . . Two adolescent girls were playing at hopscotch on the patch of tarmac. At his question they giggled, turning away and mumbled: 'No one knows where she is . . .' Puzzled, he went to ask a housewife who was hanging sheets on a line. She gave him a hostile look and spat out: 'You might at least wait until after dark for your goings-on! It's a disgrace. They'll soon be coming in broad daylight!' This retort was so unexpected that Volsky backed away, without trying to obtain an explanation. An elderly man who was reading his paper in front of a doorway responded in more or less the same way but adopted a fatherly manner. 'Try going to a dance hall, young man. You'll find lots of pretty girls to kiss there.'

Disconcerted, Volsky walked round the building, not knowing if there was some mistake about the name . . . or suspicion due to . . . He smoothed his hair and told himself that perhaps they took him for a gypsy. It all seemed increasingly mysterious.

He crossed the courtyard and sat down on the bench occupied by the blonde woman. Her hair was unkempt. 'A blonde tart,' he thought. He hesitated, gave a little cough, ventured an exaggeratedly cheerful 'Good evening'. The woman was dozing and seemed not to be aware of his presence. She was probably tipsy and kept moaning sadly. He remained beside her, irresolute, telling himself, as one does when uncertain whether to wait: but as soon as I go, Mila will appear.

The life of the building amazed him by its routine domesticity. Just a few months after the end of the war, this washing hung between two trees, the hiss of oil in a frying pan, a child crying, a tango stuttering on a scratched gramophone record. A Sunday evening, just as if there had never been those streets dotted with corpses, those little towns transformed into charred black lace . . .

A long comfortable yawn could be heard from an open window on the ground floor. Volsky felt the dull pain with which this regenerated life afflicted him. The arrogance of happiness, the vigorous indifference of the living. This world was alien to him, just like the stalls at the theatre the night before, crammed with dress uniforms. 'The victor's world . . .' Yes, the real winner is the one who knows how to forget more quickly and more scornfully than the rest.

Dusk fell, the soft, silvery transparency of northern nights. The woman had changed position, and now, her head falling on one shoulder, was murmuring snatches of rhythmic phrases, like nursery rhymes. A stocky face, flushed from sunshine and wine, her discoloured locks falling into her eyes, a trace of blurred make-up. He experienced a certain compassion for her, almost fellow feeling. He had known a few such women at the front, a bitter tenderness amid the slaughter, sham embraces and yet true enough, for that was all the man carried with him as he went to his death. Fallen women . . . Relics of war, thought Volsky, this 'blonde tart', just like that German tank with broken tracks. 'And me . . .' he admitted.

He got up, prepared to say goodbye and suddenly froze, pricked up his ears. What the woman was murmuring seemed familiar to him. Not the words but the voice itself, or rather the quality of that voice. The whispered humming through drunkenness had not varied and yet its modulation was striking, thanks to the accuracy of the nuances. 'She has a trained voice . . .' he had time to think and, already with a sharpness that took his breath away, these muted tones began conjuring up a face painfully preserved by memory.

The woman half opened her eyes. Her dull expression revealed quite different features shining through, like the image in a transfer, then lapsed into a dough of somnolence and disgust. The woman Volsky kept stored in his memory was a survivor with a trembling body, big eyes sunk deep in the ink of their sockets, a bony skull that stuck out through her skin . . . The woman, who went back to her murmuring again, had swollen features, the body of one who has overeaten after starving. And yet the old face kept reappearing, intermittently, in a rippling of light.

He took her hand and spoke in purposely neutral tones: 'It's me. Do you recognize me, my dear?' She withdrew her hand, stared at him with an uneasy look, clumsily assuming an air of offended dignity. 'I'm not your dear! I'm not just anyone, you know!' The voice was at once coarse and vulnerable. He experienced a brief moment of hesitation: profit from this rebuff and leave? Return to the world of the victors . . . He moved away from the bench and saw the woman's face fade and solidify. The features whose pattern he had recognized were engulfed in sullen heaviness. Her eyelids closed, her chin sank onto her chest.

Already a few steps away, he looked back. Through the dusk he saw a woman all alone beneath a sky that seemed to be there only for her. No sound, as if the inhabitants of the building had disappeared. Trees motionless. This woman in a darkness where everything lived on hold. And where no thought could be hidden.

He went back to the bench, crouched down and sang softly as if crooning a lullaby. 'To you, my beloved, I shall confide my dream . . .' His memory prompted him with the words that came next. He sang a little louder and was not surprised when the woman's lips responded to him. Her eyes were closed, she was smiling softly, allowing that other being to sing who was awakening within her. Volsky helped her to get up. She walked beside him, still sunk in her melodious lethargy.

Several hours of that pale night sufficed for Mila to tell him what she had lived through since their last concert. If she had wept in recounting it, uttered cries of distress, her story would, doubtless, have been less painful to listen to. But she went behind a screen and a moment later Volsky saw a woman who bore little resemblance to the tipsy 'blonde tart' of a moment earlier. After she had splashed her face with cold water it became more refined, her hair drawn back onto her neck gave her features the look of someone facing a powerful, icy night wind. The trace of an old scar marked the top of her brow. On a wall he noticed several drawings, doubtless made by children, and a sketch: a woman with dark hair, a very thin face and great, shadowed eyes . . . The woman who sat down before him now bore a resemblance to this drawing.

They did not switch on the light, contenting themselves with the bluish luminescence filtering through the window, and the red glow of the little stove beneath a kettle (both of them referred to plain boiled water as 'tea', for this was the tea they used to drink during the blockade: and the word became their first sign of recognition).

'The last time we saw one another was in December,

you know, at our concert . . . But after that things became worse than ever . . .'

She spoke calmly, no sighs, no tears. 'Worse than ever,' he repeated mentally. 'No. Worse could only be death. And we stayed alive.' He wanted to say this, so that Mila's voice should relax, but the doomed city he had known was already taking shape in her account and the more she spoke, the more he realized he did not know everything, not this other frontier, beyond life.

Yet there was nothing new in Mila's recollections: two million human beings waiting to die in a city that was an architectural fairyland. He saw this young woman leaving hospital, with a bandaged forehead, embarking on a long journey across Leningrad to reach the flat they had left a week before. One had to imagine her hunger, her attempts to light the fire and even, perhaps, her emotion at the sight of a scarf of his, hanging from a hook on the door.

There was nothing surprising either in the existence of the children who came to Mila's during the great frosts in January. First of all, twins aged twelve, a brother and sister, whose mother had just died. Then a much younger child, possibly five, who remained obstinately silent by day but emitted screams of horror in his sleep. Another, with bright red hair and the nickname 'Mandarin', boasted, at the age of eight and a half, of having run away from his orphanage twice. 'And now they've *evasculated* the orphanage. And they've forgotten all about me . . .' Mila guessed that he had taken advantage of the evacuation to do a bunk yet again. Mandarin's vitality was disconcerting, as was his constant good humour. He was the one who taught the others to eat sunshine. The ravenous children would sit in a row facing the window embellished with hoar frost, open their mouths and bite into the light illuminating their pale faces, pretending to chew, to swallow . . . Among these stray children there was also a boy with transparent skin, his eyelids always a little lowered, for whom it was a great effort to speak. This languid air contrasted oddly with the brisk resonance of his name in Russian, Edward. Mila noticed that, though generally in the background, he became extremely alert at the time when their bread ration was being shared out, eager to obtain a little more than the others . . . Almost every week another child would come to join the 'family'. At the end of January Mila brought two little girls in from the street, the elder was carrying her sister like a mother carrying her baby.

Shortly after this their small tribe moved to other quarters. Mila decided to house the children in that empty workers' hostel on the outskirts of Leningrad. The centre of the city was being bombed far more, the suburbs were left alone. Wood for heating was easy to find in that great deserted building. But, above all, on the road that ran beside that district one could beg for bread from soldiers going to or returning from the front.

As with the lives of everyone in that dying city, whether they survived or not could be a matter of several

159

extra degrees of frost, a fall in the street just before collecting your slice of bread, extra tiredness which could suddenly shatter the body. And above all, the chance of that scrap of food which might or might not be tossed out from an army lorry. Yes, one little mishap was enough to threaten the existence of her 'family', which already comprised sixteen children.

It was not just one mishap but a whole sequence of events, taken together, on one particular day, that became fateful. On her way back from the city Mila slipped and twisted her ankle. The next day she was unable to go and beg for bread at the roadside. That night, after a week of thaw, the winter unleashed a bliz-zard which covered the footpaths linking the hostel to the rest of the district in three feet of snow. Several of her children were no longer getting up and only Mandarin remained lively and merry. He helped her to light the stove and called out to the others. 'Come on, stir your stumps, you bunch of lazybones! I'm going to show you how to eat fire . . .' Some of them, roused by his energy, dragged themselves over to the stove and imitated him, opening their mouths to bite into the warmth given off by the flames.

'He's indestructible, that one,' thought Mila, watching Mandarin's red head bobbing up, now in the entrance hall, now in the dormitory installed around the stove.

And yet it was him she found one evening stretched out in the corridor with a fixed stare, his body frozen. He was gasping for breath, then, when carried close to the fire, he managed to whisper: 'I've got bells ringing in my chest . . .' The last scraps of bread had been eaten the day before.

She went out and, after an hour of wading through the snow, reached the road. For the first time she did not have the strength to remain upright, collapsed against a street light, waited, no longer able to feel her hands in her mittens or her frozen feet in her felt boots. A lorry appeared, she rushed out, barred its way, resolved to snatch what food there was from the people it was carrying to the front. The driver jumped down off the running board, advanced through the snow flurry, ready to knock aside this phantom that was obstructing him. 'Sixteen kids. Nothing to eat for two days . . .' she stammered. The soldier replied in a voice shredded by the wind: 'Fifty-two corpses in the lorry. We're eating dead horses. I can give you tobacco, nothing else . . .'

Next morning she was able to bring back a few slices of bread from the city. She heated the water, prepared to throw the crusts in to make a brew intended for the whole household . . . While she was getting the bowls ready the bread disappeared. The child who was eating it (it was Edward) did not hide himself, looked at her like an animal that knows it has done wrong. She slapped him, yelled oaths never uttered in front of children, wept. Then went rigid, helpless, staring at this young face disfigured by fear and the instinct to survive. Still chewing, he sniffled: 'I was very hungry . . . My uncle works in the Party administration.' These words disarmed her, so absurd did this reference to the apparatus of power sound coming from a boy of eleven standing at a table where there were still several crumbs of bread left. She knew he was lying. With a highly placed uncle he would not have been there among these lost children. He must have heard someone using the phrase, sensed the weight of authority that lay behind it, and repeated it like a parrot, hoping for privileged treatment. Other children, attracted by the smell of bread, were busy nibbling at the crumbs in the expectation of a meal.

That evening those who could get up arranged themselves around the fire to 'eat' some, as Mandarin had taught them. He himself, huddled in a corner, kept giving little coughs, as if he were trying to speak and could not manage it. She sat beside him, adjusted a woollen cap that had slipped off his head. He opened his eyes, at first with a glazed look, then recognized her, tried to smile. 'Don't worry, Mandarin. Tomorrow I'll go to the city. I'll bring some bread and maybe even some flour . . .' She broke off, for he was screwing up his eyes like someone who wants to save another person from telling a white lie. It was an adult's expression and it was also in a very adult voice that he whispered: 'Auntie Mila, I'm going to die tonight. You can give my bread to the children . . .' The dissonance between this little body and the grave voice gave her a start. She began scolding the boy, shaking him: 'What nonsense! Tomorrow I'll make some proper soup for you . . .' Seeing that he had closed his eyes to spare her these useless words of encouragement, she fell silent . . .

Half an hour later she was at her lookout post beside a bend in the road that led to the front.

There was a limpid, dark sky, swept clean by the great north wind. The frozen road crunched beneath her feet like broken glass. She knew that in cold like this a starving person does not live long. The notion came to her of going right to the soldiers' camp and stealing bread from them. The notion of a madwoman. Or else it was the world that was mad, for there was this child who had just calmly said: 'I'm going to die tonight . . .' She felt ready to do anything to snatch a bit of food from this world. The instinct of a she-wolf that will get killed to save its young. She even thought herself capable of crossing the front line to go and ask the Germans for bread. A vision of a trade-off passed through her mind, herself taking food for the children and then returning to the enemy soldiers to be beaten, violated, killed, happy that her own body, her own life were utterly unimportant.

After walking for twenty minutes she stopped, having stumbled several times. If she fell she would not be able to get up again and the cold was already making her movements stiff. Without her the children were doomed. She had to go back. The star-studded sky was magnificent, funereal. She paused for a few seconds, her gaze lost in its dark splendour and in lieu of a prayer, made this vow: bread for the children and no matter what suffering for me.

The headlights of a jeep blinded her just as she was opening the door to the hostel. An army officer called out to her, but before noticing his huge frame and his greatcoat, unbuttoned despite the cold, what she noticed, to the point of being made giddy, was the aroma of food emanating from his mouth, as well as a strong smell of alcohol. 'Would you have a glass of water for me, darling? My soul's on fire!' He bent over and the breath of this man who had just eaten well caught her by the throat. She led him into the kitchen, offered him water, spoke about the children. 'Oh, that can be fixed. I've got sausage and bread in the van. I'm the most important man in the city. I supply Smolny.' He got her to give him another glass of water, snorted contentedly and began describing the foodstuffs he delivered to the city's top brass.

Mila was hardly listening to him, picturing a large pot on the fire, slices of sausage in a broth thickened with flour and the happy clatter of spoons.

'Maybe I could have a little flour as well,' she murmured, overcome with giddiness from inhaling the smell of meat given off by this man.

'Oh yes. You can have it all, darling, thanks to your pretty face!' He grasped her arm, pulled her towards him. 'But I've got sixteen kids here, and several of them are ill . . .' she tried to explain, breaking free.

'Oh, so you don't trust me. Me, a general staff officer!' He was on the brink of losing his temper, then, overcome by lust, he changed his tactics. 'Hold on. You shall see it with your own eyes!'

He went out to the vehicle and came back carrying a canvas sack. With a salesman's gesture he opened it in front of Mila: two large tins of food, a packet of meal, a round loaf . . .

'There you are, darling. It's just as I said. If you're nice to me . . .' He embraced her, breathing words into her face that reeked of stale food and alcohol. A tremulous, inaudible protest formed within her as the man pushed her over to a bedframe. 'One of the children told me he's going to die tonight. You should be ashamed . . .'

No, she must explain nothing, simply contrive to be non-existent. To repress the nausea brought on by this mouth stinking of satiety, not to feel this hand brutally burrowing into her body . . . She managed to be no longer herself right up to the last gasp of pleasure from the man taking her. Until he left in a flurry of guffaws and promises.

She remained in this non-existent state as she prepared the meal. The children came running, ate in silence, went back to bed. In the sack left by the army man she found a bottle of vodka, drank straight from the bottle and when drunkenness came, finally allowed herself to weep.

Two days later Mandarin appeared beside the fire, as merry as before. No, not as before. Now his eyes were smiling through the veil of death.

One evening the soldier returned. And everything was repeated: food against a few minutes of non-existence. And the vodka afterwards, which quickly settled the argument between shame and the spirit of sacrifice.

There were other visits, other men, and always this extremely simple barter: the children's survival assured by a moment of anonymous pleasure. During the

165

March snowstorms and the thaw she would not, in any case, have been able to get to her lookout post or to reach the city, where there were fewer and fewer people left alive.

She did not know when she was driven out of her own life. Possibly that day in May in front of a mirror when she did not recognize herself. Or else during the following winter: the taste of vodka became essential to her without there being any nocturnal visit.

At all events, when peace returned, she became that other woman ('a loose woman', the neighbours called her) living in a room in a hostel, a building occupied by new arrivals. Her children were put into an orphanage; she remained alone, buried in a past where everything reminded her of the blockade, in an alcoholic stupor which made her indifferent to the coarseness of the men who called on her.

One evening (the whole building was celebrating the victory over Germany), she was sitting outside her window and suddenly into her memory overcome by drunkenness came words from a life now destroyed: 'To you, my beloved, I shall confide my dream . . .' She sobbed so violently that even the hubbub of a celebration party broke off. One woman exclaimed in indignant tones: 'Just listen to that! Everyone's singing for joy and all that scrubber can do is howl her head off . . .'

This was doubtless the moment when she turned into what people now saw her as. Shortly after that she bleached her dark hair and even had this comforting thought: 'If I die now no one will recognize me.' She realized that what she dreaded most was encountering once more the man who had sung: 'To you, my beloved . . .'

A moth hurtled towards the flame of the stove, Volsky waved his hand to drive it away, to save it, and this gesture broke the stillness that Mila's words had imposed on them.

'That's how it was, my life,' she said in a toneless voice. 'I hoped you wouldn't find me again . . . There are lots of women on their own now. Soldiers coming back have plenty of choice . . .'

'Well I have found you again. You can see I have.'

She seemed not to have heard.

'I even dreamed that you died in battle. I knew your grave and I used to go there. And that way you couldn't see what I've become . . .'

He smiled, in spite of himself.

'Very sorry. I'm afraid I wasn't killed . . . And you haven't changed so much . . .'

'There's no point in lying, Georgy. You know very well what I've become. A whore.'

He drew a breath, preparing to utter a retort, but let out only an abrupt sigh. And all at once, dreading the return of silence, spoke very quickly and with great agitation.

'All right. Agreed. A whore. But in that case, I'm a killer! Yes, I've often killed. That was my job in the war. This red star, you see, they stuck it on me to thank me for having assassinated thousands of Germans. I spent four years killing men. I tried to hit as many as possible and when I got to the trenches I'd just been pounding, what I saw there was a bloody pulp . . . I wasn't made for this profession. I loved singing, you know. And I spent four years yelling orders at soldiers, telling them to fire faster, to kill more. Then one day . . . I chose not to shoot down a German soldier from a tank unit. I could have done it. I was armed, he wasn't. I didn't shoot. Because—'

His voice broke off in a shrill cry. And in response to this wail an angry hammering suddenly resounded at their door and a female duet let fly in a burst of oaths and shrieks: 'Just you stop that racket or I'll call the militia! That cow has them coming in at two o'clock in the morning now . . .'

The aggressiveness of the attack brought them close to one another, the viperish hissing prompted them to stand up, in a defensive movement, their bodies drawn together, their arms reaching towards an embrace.

'For I realized,' he whispered, in almost joyful tones, 'that if I'd fired at that young German then I really would have become a killer. And for you, it's the same. It's clearer still, even . . .'

He fell silent for fear of shattering this understanding, which suddenly had no need of words. It had not been pity that had held him back from killing. Simply, at that moment he had viewed the world (and the German and himself and the whole earth) with a perception that was immeasurably greater than his own. The same perception that the woman had had in exchanging her body for bread.

'I was thinking of making up the bed for you, but . . .' murmured Mila and smiled, as if the notion now seemed pointless to her.

Once again, without explaining anything, they understood that they must leave. Go away before this world woke up and continued with a life from which they were forever excluded.

Their preparations were swift. Mila seemed amazed at how few belongings she possessed. Some clothes, three chipped plates, a kettle. And her children's drawings, the pieces of paper she took down from the wall around the stove.

They went out, crossed the courtyard, as if on the edge of a waking dream. A tumble of clouds in the sky, a wind losing itself in the drowsy rustling of leaves. A child's garment trailing in the grass beneath a line where shirts and sheets billowed. Mila picked it up, fastened it with a clothes peg . . . They turned to look back. Behind the dark windows a strange innocence could be sensed: the sleep of those people, so certain of their truths, so easy-going, so hard. And with no notion of what this workers' hostel had been for the couple who were leaving it.

The road followed the stages they knew: the corner where Mila used to wait for the lorries, then the place where their choir had given its last concert . . . They walked beside the river. Above its swirling waters the sky was beginning to grow light. From time to time they had to skirt craters left by bombs. Some of

170

these were filled with water and already bristling with rushes, from which birds arose in flight.

Just as they were passing a little collapsed bridge Mila slowed down, suggested that they make a halt. And it was then that they saw an undamaged house on the slope of the valley, away from the roofs destroyed by fire. An empty *izba* with a wide open door. A poplar tree some forty feet high stood between a wooden fence and the coping of a well. The violet pallor of the morning gave the illusion that the walls were transparent and the house was gently rocking, like a vessel on the ocean swell of the tall grasses.

IV

People found their life as a couple completely ordinary. An old *izba* without electricity, among ruins? But after the war half the country was living like that. Always dressed in the same worn clothes? But there was little elegance in the Russia of those years. Nor was there anything unusual about the work they did: Mila taught music at the school in the neighbouring small town, Volsky found work as a postman. People got used to their self-effacing presence. They saw the woman going in at the school entrance early in the morning, they noticed the man as he cycled past, his big sack filled with good or bad news. People spoke to them, they would reply politely but were not forthcoming. Besides, who was forthcoming in those days when an incautious word could cost talkative people dear?

If the truth be told, their only distinctive feature was the colour of their hair: over a few months the man's lost its sombre hue and turned white and the woman's dark tresses reappeared. But this curiosity caused little surprise. The towns were full of war-wounded, disfigured faces . . . Yes, a commonplace couple.

What seemed more unusual was the spot where they had settled. Hidden in the valley and the woods along its slopes were minefields, often indicated by plywood signs, occasionally not. And the earth was heavy with the bodies of soldiers.

On one of the first days after they moved in they went back to the site of their last concert. Volsky walked down towards the river and there was a sudden sharp, metallic clatter beneath his foot. He bent down and searched among the plant stems . . . And withdrew a cymbal stained with mud and eaten into by verdigris. Mila fingered the tarnished disc. The sound set off long reverberating echoes . . . It was a hot, sweetly lazy summer's day, one made up of languid forgetfulness. They looked at one another, the same memory in the depths of their eyes: the end of a winter's night, the icy expanse from which the soldiers are mounting an attack. That singing in defiance of death. And this cymbal falling, rolling across the snow, down towards the river . . .

Their true life would be this invisible journey against the current of the time mankind lives by.

One evening, on a return visit to Leningrad, they went up into the block of flats that Volsky had lived in before the war. On the top landing the violet of the sky came spilling in at the window, a star glittered through a heat haze . . . In the courtyard the children were scuffling around a ball. Behind the door of a communal flat two housewives were arguing about the oven. A couple in their Sunday best walked down the stairs talking about a comedy that had just been released at the cinema. Life . . . Volsky and Mila exchanged glances. Yes, the life they no longer had to lead.

Their thoughts returned more than once to this freedom of theirs not to live like other people. One day, back in the city, they stopped under the windows of the Conservatoire where they had trained. A joyous tumult of notes and snatches of song poured forth over them in a flood of memories. 'A musical box . . . going off the rails,' said Mila and they smiled. The students hurrying down the front steps looked just like little figures spilling out from the tiny revolving stage. Once again Volsky and Mila felt they had been rescued from a life they might have lived by mistake.

Another musical box was the opera they went to one evening. The actors dressed up as soldiers sang of feats of arms, heroism, the motherland. The ingenious way the war had been put on the stage left Volsky perplexed. There was no mention of their own past but here, on a heavy stage set, with a background of cardboard cut-out flames, voices celebrated the defence of Leningrad in vibrant, wordy arias. At the climax an actor appeared in the role of one of the Party leaders. 'The Ci-i-ity of Lenin shall ne-ver fa-a-all!' he sang. He was a big fat man, wearing a uniform too tight for his portly figure. 'The thighs of the King in *Rigoletto* . . .' Volsky recalled.

After the performance they took a tram, which

dropped them at the gates of the city. From there the way was familiar. Two hours of walking along roads damaged by bombing, then through sleeping fields beside the Lukhta. In the still night the rustle of plants on the banks of the river could be heard. In unison with this, Volsky was softly murmuring the simple words he used to sing at the front, when marching along in a column of soldiers. Their house appeared, tinged with blue by the twinkling dark of the sky: small, stuck there lopsidedly on a hillside beneath the immense arrow of a poplar.

'Mila will soon have had enough of this shack of ours,' he thought. 'She'll come to be envious of those people at the theatre who went quietly home tonight instead of trekking through the fields like us . . .'

She stopped, pointed at their house. 'Look. It's as if someone's waiting for us.' One of the window panes had caught the gilding of the moon, a discreet and patient light, like a lamp placed there to show the way through the darkness.

During the months that followed they only returned to the city once, when Mila wanted to see 'her children' again. It was the day of the first snowfall.

Behind the railings at the orphanage shadowy figures seemed to be waltzing, elated by the dance of the snowflakes. Mila recognized faces, whispered names . . . A little apart from his comrades stood a boy of about twelve and, with his head thrown back, his eyes half closed, he was holding up his face to the white flurries.

Suddenly overcome with giddiness, he stumbled and his *shapka* fell off, revealing bright red hair, cut very short. He retrieved it and as he stood up, noticed this couple standing on the other side of the railings. Mila turned away, began walking with her head bowed, Volsky followed her. After a silence he suggested in an uncertain voice: 'What if we took him to live with us? And the others too . . .'

They did not mention it again but from then on their house seemed to be inhabited by this expectation.

Mine-clearance operations had begun in August and lasted for a whole month. It was as if the sappers were unravelling a vast spider's web around the little *izba*. It was striking to see how many tons of death the two armies had succeeded in burying. Every footpath was stuffed with it. Every forest glade was a trap for an unwary footstep . . .

As they were leaving, one of the sappers took them up to the top of the slope and showed them a vast hummocky area. 'That's not mines there,' he said. 'Those are graves. But we're not to do anything about them . . .'

Graves, contrived in a hurry, after battles. Yes, little stray mounds lost amid the folds in the ground. Here and there a name was preserved on a sign fastened to a post, the only record of a life, but the mounds were mostly mute. Closer to the ridge above the bank they found bones covered in mud and dead plants.

What they would end up accomplishing began with

almost random acts: picking up a pistol in a collapsed trench, a notebook with its pages eaten away by damp which made it impossible to read . . . They gave themselves no plan of action, they imposed on themselves no ritual solemnity. Quite simply, day after day, they were trying to rescue from oblivion those whom they had seen shot down during their last concert.

Only once did they wonder what should be done with the mortal remains. For there were relics of German soldiers too. Helmets, the shreds of uniforms, bones, skulls . . . There was still bitter hatred, sustained by memories of the stranglehold on Leningrad, the towns razed to the ground that Volsky had passed through, by that immense bloodbath that Russia had become. 'All those children who died because of him,' thought Mila as she touched a skull with the edge of her spade. Hatred seemed as natural as breathing. Yet the air they breathed was tinged with the acrid scent of russet leaves, the chill of the hoar frost whose crystals shone like rainbows in the sun. On the ground the last flowers, burned by the frost, rose up among the bones. And from the pale, luminous sky there emanated a gentle aura of convalescence.

'What are we going to do with all this?' grunted Volsky. 'Chuck it into a gully and forget about it?'

Mila shook her head gently. 'I don't know . . . They took us for savages. Animals to be exterminated. I think they should be buried the same as ours. With names, if possible. That will prove they were wrong about us.'

They did it, extending the rows of mounds, planting a young sapling brought by Volsky from the forest beside each grave. At the start of the autumn they learned that the Museum of the Blockade had just been opened in Leningrad. They deposited there all that they had found during their funerary work: weapons, documents, decorations. And even a letter, preserved thanks to the silver paper wrapping from a bar of chocolate. Words of tenderness written by a German soldier . . .

In spring this cemetery would already have the look of a spinney, shining with young leaves.

From the ruins of the village Volsky collected a good amount of undamaged timber. Logs, planks, beams, the wherewithal for extending their little hut. 'Two more large rooms,' they planned, picturing the children moving in. This future home was being sketched in their minds with a fine line of light.

Their own life together was like a subtle watercolour sketch, invisible to other people. They gave the world what it required of them and for the rest of the time were content to be forgotten. Mila could be seen emerging from the school, the sleeves of her dress white with chalk. Volsky could be observed cycling along the rutted roads, his postman's sack on his back.

And one October day they could be seen running along a station platform in Leningrad, from which a local train was leaving, the only one finally put back in service. They just missed it, stopped, breathless, and saw all kinds of looks at the passing carriage windows, mocking, indifferent, sympathetic. But nobody could guess at the true lives of this couple as they retraced their footsteps, crossed the city and left it on foot, following a familiar road.

Nobody knew that they had come to bring the last relics that the earth of the graves had yielded up to them. At the Blockade Museum they had felt a great peace, mingled with bitterness. The rooms, which still resembled those in an ordinary warehouse, contained a jumble of tragic fragments from the past, from those years it was so hard to talk about. Photos, personal items, letters, exercise books in which children dying of hunger had drawn grass, clouds in summer . . . And the notebook belonging to that child who wrote down the date when each member of her family died.

In the middle of one room the Luftwaffe aircraft shot down over Leningrad loomed large.

The peace they experienced came from saving these fragments of truth from oblivion. But also from the gold of the leaves covering the muddy road. They walked on, happy to have missed the train and to be making their way through a luminous mist redolent of the cool of forest undergrowth. And their joy came from this perception: despite the boundless suffering concentrated in the rooms at the museum, there was still this misty day with its muted light and the pearly droplets on the woman's eyelashes and the man's smile, a fleeting smile, no longer to be confused with the grimacing scar from his wound.

No one could guess at this life of theirs that took its course through the fragile tenacity of such moments.

This humble beauty had no need of the fun and games set in motion by the end of the war. Parades, processions, speeches glorifying the Leader who had guided the people to victory. And the desire some had to play a leading role in these victory celebrations.

They kept apart from this hubbub. Thanks to their solitude, their love. Thanks to the measured resonance they became aware of one December day in the snow-covered forest where they were collecting fallen timber. The wind blew strongly above the tops of the tall fir trees. But down below, seated on their bundle of firewood, all they could make out was a rustling sound: a mass of snow came tumbling down from the treetops and as it slid from one branch to the next, found time to whisper a brief sequence of words. They did not speak, surprised to see how simple, almost poor, happiness could be; yes, materially poor and yet so abundant. A pile of snow embarked on its slippery descent down the branches, gave off a rapid whispering, fell. And the silent forest seemed to sense the presence of the woman tilting her face, eyes closed, towards the lazy fluttering of the snowflakes . . . Men had ripped open this earth with trenches, thought Volsky, had buried thousands of mines and then set about killing one another and the massacre had lasted four long years, and when it was over the survivors dug up the mines and went away. And the forest has once more become as it was before the killing. 'And now the woman I love has her eyes closed, listening to the wind, and snow crystals settle on her face. A face which resembles that of a very thin young woman, with dark hair, drawn by a child . . .'

That December evening they tried out the big stove Volsky had built between the two new rooms of their house for the first time. The branches blazed with

184

cheerful ferocity and they pictured Mila's children seated in a circle, holding out their hands towards the fire.

When the snows melted the water came right up to the front steps of their house and they laughed as, without walking down them, Volsky flung an old piece of fishing net he had found in the loft into this slow tide. A scent of the damp bark of alder trees hung in the air, the warmth of wooden walls heated by the sun. Perched at the top of the steps, they watched the sky slowly turning pale, reflected in the river, and from time to time noticed the bobbing of the floats above the net. In the distance, beyond the waters, the other bank could be made out, and the delicate silhouettes of the trees now watching over the graves.

One glance took it all in. The riverbank where they had seen so many men die. And the river, slow and broad as a lake now, where once the ice had been streaked with the blood of a wounded man crawling up towards the singers. And their voices mingled with the shouting and explosions. A past still so close to the wooden steps where a woman now sat tossing twigs into the water gilded by the setting sun . . .

'So what was the point of it all?' thought Volsky, and in his memory he saw again those men busily clustered around a gun. There, on the same shore. Men who killed or were killed. What was the point?

'The defence of the country, victory . . .' the words proclaimed their harsh truth within himself. All those

185

deaths were necessary. And often heroic. 'Yes, useful, but only because people are unaware of this happiness,' he said to himself and once more sensed the approach of a truth that encompassed all men and all lives. The happiness of watching these twigs floating away on the current lit by a low sun. Of seeing this woman stand up, go into the house. The happiness of seeing her face at a window above the waters. Her smile, the glow of her dress perceived through a window pane.

This happiness rendered absurd men's desire to dominate, to kill, to possess, thought Volsky. For neither Mila nor he possessed anything. Their joy came from the things one does not possess, from what other people had abandoned or scorned. But, above all, this sunset, this scent of warm bark, these clouds above the young trees in the graveyard, these belonged to everybody!

The fisherman's net, which he began to haul up onto the steps, emerged empty. From time to time, amid the meshes slipping through the water, there was a dull golden flash of moonlight.

No one around them could perceive this transfigured world. Their neighbours cursed the worse than usual flooding of the Lukhta, the waterlogged roads. Mila and Volsky would nod in agreement, so as not to vex them, but on their return home sat upon the old steps letting their gaze drift across the shining expanse. At night the waters murmured beneath their windows, little waves lapped gently against the steps. This calm and joy should be spoken of to help people live differently. But with what words?

Explain nothing, Volsky thought one day, just show this other life . . . He was returning from Leningrad and, without intending to, he witnessed the rehearsal for a parade at the edge of the city. Bearing an enormous effigy of Stalin, a procession of workers was due, according to the scenario, to meet up with a column of soldiers, so that the head of the Leader should appear above the victorious army. A band then launched into its brassy din. The merging of the two was slow to achieve the desired artistic effect. Angry shouts rang out from a wooden perch on which there was a little man in a trilby hat shouting: 'I can't see Comrade Stalin!' (The workers hoisted the portrait up as high as possible.) Or else: 'Come on! Look lively now!' The soldiers lifted up their chins, their eyes wide . . .

Volsky went pedalling on amid the fields. The barking of the loudspeaker faded, giving way to the clatter of the old bicycle. What he had seen was comic, he could have laughed at it, but sadness lingered in his mind. It would doubtless not have been difficult to find workers in the procession who had lived through the horrors of the blockade. And many among the soldiers would be those who carried within them a heavy burden of mangled bodies, faces gone forever. Such grief should have led them towards a new and luminous truth. Instead of which it was this return to the same old circus parade, these foolishly radiant faces.

He went to the school where Mila taught, stopped beneath the windows of the music room, listened. And as the children sang in chorus, recognized a song his regimental comrades used to sing between battles. He had often hummed these tunes, his voice eloquent both of the soldiers' weariness and the fragile nature of the hope they clung to, despite the mud and carnage. This was the music Mila was teaching her pupils, unusual in the school repertoire, which consisted of cheerful, patriotic outpourings.

It was a moment that gave expression to the true meaning of his new life: these faint voices which seemed to come from a daydream, a day lit up by the very first foliage, the scent of flooded woodland and, so close at hand, snatched from death, the presence of the woman he loved. The rippling movement of her arm conducting the children's singing . . .

He thought again about the war, which had brought them the wisdom of simple happiness. And became confused, unwilling to accept the terrible price for such wisdom. Mila emerged, came to kiss him. He wanted to question her: 'Why couldn't we be as happy as this before the war? From the moment we first met? When we were young and carefree?' But Mila's look was expecting other words.

'This is it. I've got it,' he said and saw a shadow of anxiety vanish from the woman's face. From his postman's sack he drew a typewritten sheet bearing several signatures and stamps. It was the licence given by the city authorities for them to adopt the orphans, 'Mila's children', as Volsky called them. The first four of them were to arrive at the start of the September term.

One evening in May it seemed as if he had fathomed the mystery of their new happiness . . . The dusk was mild; they had no desire to return home, remained lying amid the trees, beside a spring which they had cleared of scrub a week earlier. The earth was white from the petals of a wild cherry, it was like being in a winter snowstorm. The scent of this white blossom and the acrid freshness of lilies of the valley . . . 'I've lived through this before,' thought Volsky. 'Yes, in the war, after a battle. This blizzard of petals. That soldier who waved his hand, like swatting a mosquito, and then collapsed. Not a mosquito but a stray piece of shrapnel, a scrap of metal from an explosion. Heady blossom, the icy scent of lilies of the valley, a lovely

189

spring evening and that fine young man who'd just died . . .'

Volsky stared at the woman who was smiling with half-closed eyes through the slow swirl of the petals. A strange being: a woman whom this world had so many times tried to destroy, a body which, only recently, had been worn away by hunger, then a face which could no longer mimic the bone structure of a skull, a woman violated. And this had transformed her little by little into human detritus. 'These eyes of hers have been filled with death, with ice, with ugliness, and now they can see this violet sky and, amid the fistfuls of petals, a star, very close, which, in its turn, sees us . . .'

The perception he had was like a shaft of light. 'No,' he thought. 'There's no need to explain anything but simply to recognize in the other this astonishing being who goes infinitely beyond what she has lived through, and is living now, what people see in her and what the world makes of her. Recognize and love this invisible element in a woman at this very moment, beneath the petals' slow descent, this bruised body whose tenderness is still intact, these eyes whose brightness makes me alive.'

During those May days the war ended for them. One year after the end of the war.

A long time later, returning in thought to that year lived on the banks of the Lukhta, Volsky would be struck by the length of time taken by what, in fact, was only the first stage of settling in. Each of the seasons would seem like a whole lifetime. An autumn lifetime, the embroidery of the hoar frost on the gold of the dead leaves. A winter lifetime, that oil lamp at their window, a stray gleam in a snowstorm. A spring lifetime, those nights when the waters came right up to the old wooden front steps . . . And the summer, too, their house afloat on the bluish swell of the grasses and the flowers. He would remember that very slow, very intimate eternity, a single day of which could smooth away all the wounds of his broken life.

The same thought struck them both and they exchanged amused glances: this white foal, yes, with the slightly clumsy grace of infancy, the freedom of a creature still ignorant of life's barriers . . . It ran along the shore, went into the water, backed away with an abrupt caper, pranced back up the slope.

Volsky was busy repairing the roof; Mila, on a ladder, was passing him tar-coated wooden battens. From time to time they broke off, happy to see so much simultaneous activity from their lofty perch. The frisking of the foal, children bathing in the river and a little further on, beyond the willow plantations, women gathering the hay into haycocks and a very small girl amusing herself by climbing onto the precarious piles and balancing upright on them like an acrobat.

Suddenly she fell and at the same moment an explosion rang out. Beyond the trees a curtain of spurts of earth and smoke arose. The foal galloped on a few more yards before collapsing, its right flank torn away. A mine, which the sappers had failed to remove the previous autumn . . .

Volsky and Mila grasped what had happened, a rapid sequence of events: the foal galloping, the little girl falling, thrown off balance by the roar of the explosion, the frozen postures of the peasant women and finally that confusion of white and red thrashing about briefly in the dust.

The lives of other people, which they had believed they could keep at a distance, were unfolding, mingling the traces of war with the routine of peacetime, the tears of the little girl as she walked towards the dead foal with her head averted. And the children appearing from all sides, hiding their curiosity behind frightened faces. And, a little later, the *kolkhoznik* who came with a wheelbarrow, dismembered the carcass with a few blows of an axe, loaded up the meat and buried the rest in the hole left by the explosion.

They forced themselves not to see this death as a portent. For a while their own world, this fragile timelessness apart from the world, could survive. And then one day at the end of August this strange observer made his appearance. They were high on the ridge above the shore in the middle of putting up a fence round the place where the soldiers were buried. Mila was writing a name they had managed to identify on one of the grave markers . . .

She was the first to notice the strange lookout. On the opposite bank, not far from their house, stood a black car, an army officer had a huge pair of binoculars focused on the graveyard where they were working. His bizarrely static posture, his cape, excessively long in view of the fine drizzle that veiled the horizon, everything about this dumb show seemed disproportionate and menacing. It was rather like picturing a general surveying a battlefield. Another officer appeared and the statue with the binoculars stirred, shook its head and both walked towards the house. The daylight was fading but from the top of the ridge the two men could clearly be seen going up to the windows, peering inside . . .

In the time it took Volsky and Mila to go down to their boat and cross the Lukhta, the officers had gone. The only traces were a cigarette stub with a fine gold band and the imprint of a boot on the flowerbed in front of the house. 'They must have been surveyors on reconnaissance,' said Volsky, pretending to be unconcerned. 'They've probably got a map to draw up.'

For him the army officers' visit was a secret relief. As if, not having the courage to wake up from his dream and to arouse Mila, he had been helped by their appearance. The world was there, on the threshold of their love.

In referring to them as 'army officers' he had been lying, their uniform was unmistakeable. And it was Mila who remarked on it. 'It's odd, those two fellows from State Security. It reminds me of what happened the other day at school. Yes, there was an inspector . . . The head teacher told me in advance she'd be coming, so there was nothing unexpected about it. Except that she stood there, as still as a stone. Like that man spying on us with his binoculars. Then she went away without saying a word. Apparently the songs I teach the children are not ideologically correct . . .'

They were sitting on the front steps of their *izba*.

Now that the waters had subsided, the house seemed to be perched even higher above the fields and more solitary. Volsky listened, hesitated before replying: he must either attempt a reassuring tone and therefore lie, or else . . . He bowed his head and suddenly noticed another cigarette stub ringed with a band of gold among the tufts of grass. Like a gimlet eye staring at them.

'You know, Mila, I haven't mentioned this to you, but the mail I deliver—' He broke off, conscious that his voice sounded guilty, although there was no fault to confess. 'Yes, I notice more and more letters coming from prisons. I think it's started again, the purges . . .'

They said very little to one another, using the oblique turns of phrase that everyone employed at the time. One did not say 'so and so has been arrested' but 'he's had problems'. Indeed, Mila could not have said 'those fellows from State Security', that form of words would come later in Volsky's reminiscences, when it became possible to talk about it. At the time, she would simply have spoken of 'the Big House', which was how people referred to the secret police headquarters in Leningrad.

In a few more or less coded words, they said it all to one another: the waves of arrests unleashed to an extent worse than ever before, the fear that, after a brief relaxation at the end of the war, was turning faces to stone again, the suspicion that marked every word. The victory over the Nazis had freed the hands of the local persecutors, now eager to make the people pay for their own cowardice.

Mentioning two or three details about each of the individuals who had disappeared, Volsky and Mila recalled those who had 'had problems': people living in the neighbouring small town, old friends in Leningrad. Already a long litany of ghosts. They knew people chose different tactics for survival. Some pretended to notice nothing, talked, went to work, smiled at their families, sleepwalking like torpid automatons. Others transformed their lives into the waiting of a condemned man, rehearsing in soliloquy the arguments they believed would prove their innocence, slept fully dressed, knowing that arrests took place at night. Sometimes they went mad. Yet others attempted to defuse the threat by mocking it.

'My father did that.' Volsky realized he was talking about this for the first time. 'In the days of collectivization in our village, if they found a bag of corn hidden in a peasant's house the fellow was shot. Soon it was enough that you hadn't declared a tool or a dozen eggs. I was still a child but I remember the day very well. It was winter, you know, freezing cold. My father went out without his coat, barefoot in the snow, and carried the only pair of boots he had left to the Expropriation Committee. He managed to adopt a very serious, almost fervent expression: 'I'm giving everything I have for the building of socialism!' The Party bosses were terribly embarrassed by fervour like this. In the end they decided he wasn't all there. They gave him back his boots and left us alone . . . Sometimes being mad could save you.'

'My father was saved by dying.'

Mila murmured this, echoing Volsky's words and at once, seeing his puzzled look, hastened to explain.

'He was an officer in Mongolia in 1939. He took part in the battle of Khalkhyn Gol. One day, when he was talking to a man he thought was his best friend, he ventured a piece of black humour: "If you ask me, there are more army officers in the camps than we have here in our ranks." Some throwaway remark like that. The commanding officer summoned him and told him to prepare himself for the worst. The next day during the assault on the Japanese he was the first to be shot down. The truth is he got himself killed. One of his comrades told us about his death. The people who were supposed to arrest him came back empty-handed: instead of apprehending an enemy of the people, they were confronted with an officer fallen on the field of battle, almost a hero. After that they left my mother and myself alone as well.'

It had all been said. The two stories, they knew, summed up the country in which they lived. Its fears, its wars, the defenceless nakedness of private existence, the impossibility of sharing one's distress. The extreme difficulty of having faith in human goodness and at the same time the awareness that only this faith could still save. A country where millions of people woke in the night, listening to the hiss of tyres on the asphalt: is that car going past? Or is it stopping outside?

'You've never talked to me about your father . . .' said Volsky, as if in reproachful tones.

'We never had time . . . Besides, if we'd started thinking about all that, we'd not have had the will to go on living.'

Volsky's first impulse was to object, to invoke the

need to bring the truth out in the open. But he thought better of it, sensing in Mila's words a truth at once more humble and almost arrogant in its frankness. She smiled. 'We wouldn't even have been able to act at the theatre. Remember: "To you, my beloved, I shall confide my dreams . . ." It was partly those songs that helped us to survive. And so many people with us!'

Thirty years later Volsky would reflect that this, too, had been his country: a couple who had been through hell, whose lives were now caught in the lens of a pair of binoculars, as if in a marksman's sights; yes, this pair of lovers seated on the front steps of an *izba*, in the pale light of an August evening, gazing at a ridge punctuated with graves above a riverbank, softly singing light melodies from an ancient, old-fashioned operetta.

They often talked now about those performances given during the blockade, the audience shivering in the darkness, Porthos singing, his face bathed in tears, actors collapsing on stage, exhausted with cold and hunger. Those wartime days became their strength, their courage, and when they pictured that last concert under gunfire, all fears seemed to them ludicrous: those two agents from Security come to spy on them? A single minute of that concert was far more daunting than any other threat.

Thinking about the children they were going to house also helped them not to live in the humiliation of fear. Constructing a bed, cutting a shirt out of an old sheet, the routine nature of such actions linked them to a future in which young lives would take possession of these objects, render them useful, alive. And when they recalled from what depths of unhappiness these children would be coming to them, those two agents with their binoculars just seemed like pantomime villains.

One evening they set up a big screen that was to divide the dormitory in two. Handling the slippery fabrics reminded them of the curtain going up and the idea arose, like a spark, in their exchanged glances: they should teach the children to act in a play, yes, to make theatre – and sing in an operetta, why not?

To the very end they resisted fear. And when, on one occasion, Volsky happened upon a cigarette stub with a gilded ring among the graves in the cemetery, he trampled this menacing token with scorn and gave a laugh: 'The Germans used to smoke elegant gaspers like that, too.'

So they did not live through the sleepless nights that so many people underwent, on the alert for the hiss of tyres outside the entrance to their building. The danger they braved erupted in broad daylight, in a huge uproar of curses, gesticulating hands, absurdly angry faces. A far cry from the silent, sly terror slowly seeping into everyone's spirits.

On this September day Mila went into Leningrad to hand in a notebook at the Blockade Museum: it had been found on a sandy slope by the shore, notes in German. When she made her way into the courtyard of the building she thought at first it must be a fire, then an anarchic demolition site, then a brawl taking place amid a conflagration. It was all these things at once. A bonfire was blazing in front of the entrance to the ware-house which served as the exhibition hall. Military personnel (those 'army officers' from State Security) were actively thrusting back the employees of the museum who seemed to be trying to leap into the flames. There was little shouting and this absence of words made the scene all the more distressing. But these women were not trying to immolate themselves, their hands were reaching into the fire to extract objects in order to save them. And the agents of State Security were hurling humble items into the blaze, which they had just snatched from the exhibition hall: bundles of letters, clothes, photographs . . . The struggle was fierce. Elderly women were battling against a wall of fists and rifle butts, falling, picking themselves up, rushing towards the fire.

It was not the bloodiest day in the history of the regime holding sway in that country. It was its day of greatest shame. And when, decades later, they opened the archives on the killings and repressions, they did not always dare to mention this deadly bonfire . . .

Mila was not aware how she found herself in the middle of the battle. She felt the scorching of the flames on her hands, her lips were bleeding, one sleeve of her dress dangled, half torn off. The heavy pounding of male fists thrust her back, she crouched, forced a way out for herself, seized a book, a photograph, tried to protect them, to hide them. An unfamiliar joy was mingled with the frenzy of this salvage operation: no protest had ever arisen in the country against the monolith of these dark uniforms and here the very first rebellion saw these women rising up, their bodies emaciated by the years of war, survivors with the angular faces of starved women.

Hysterical shouting suddenly broke out at the exhibition hall's exit. A plump man of small stature appeared, surrounded by his entourage. Mila quickly recognized him from official portraits in the newspapers: Malenkov, a member of the Leader's praetorian guard. The uniforms stood to attention, breaking off the massacre.

'Aha! The factionalists in hiding!' he bellowed.

'They've spun themselves a web of rampant reaction here! They've fabricated the myth of a Leningrad fighting all alone, without the leadership of the Party! They've left out the vital role of the great Stalin, father of our victory! Everyone out! All this stale rubbish to the fire! Quick! Move!'

The uniforms went into action again and this time, assisted by Malenkov's henchmen, they seized the staff and hurled them into a van waiting in the street. Mila grasped a bundle of letters and escaped, taking advantage of a thick trail of smoke given off by the flames as they devoured fresh armfuls of documents.

She went home on foot, had time to tell Volsky everything. And to say what people who loved one another used to say in those days: 'If anything happens to me, promise me you'll live your life without looking back at the past . . .' They revealed nothing as they took their supper with the children (the first four had moved in two weeks previously). For a while they even hoped the arrest would take place at night or else in the morning, when the children were at school . . .

They came looking for her an hour later: a car of the same type as before, they were nicknamed 'black crows', the same uniforms. Volsky came out first and it was him they spread-eagled brutally across the bonnet. The second car arrived, the agents emerging from it snatched the little case from Mila's hands that she planned to take with her. 'Look at what's inside, it's very important,' she shouted and while the two agents, intrigued, were rummaging through the few items of clothing and toiletries, she threw herself towards Volsky, they kissed and, despite the arms already separating them, succeeded in whispering a few words: 'Every day look at the sky, at least for a moment. I'll do the same . . .' They were each thrown into one of the cars. Volsky could not remember which of them, himself or Mila, had suggested looking at the sky, knowing that the other would also see it. He just had the bitter taste of blood in his mouth, Mila's lips were still bleeding.

The cars drove away with absurd haste along the earth road that led round the house. For several seconds Mila and Volsky saw a youth running after this black motorcade, waving his arms and shouting, as if he wanted to catch up with it. In the pale light of the evening his red hair glowed like a cluster of fruits on a service tree.

The hardest moment after the arrest was this interrogation. The investigating officer was young but knew that, whatever the prisoner's attitude, he must hit him. Only he was not yet in full command of torture techniques. He struck clumsily and too hard. Volsky, his hands tied behind his back, fell, pressing his head against one shoulder to hide his face. Inexplicably the blows stopped. He turned to look at the officer and could not repress an 'oh' of surprise. The man was standing upright, his head thrown back, pinching his nostrils, his fingers spotted with blood. 'Open the window, take a little ice . . .' suggested Volsky in a deliberately neutral voice. The officer snorted a kind of oath but, strangely, obeyed. The interrogation room was in the cellar, a basement window, protected by thick bars, looked out onto a pavement covered in fresh snow. The officer opened it, seized a fistful of flakes, pressed it against his nose. The bleeding calmed down and Volsky sensed that moment when a human mind wavers between compassion and scorn. He was to experience this several times during his years in the camp.

A rapid sequence of expressions passed across the young officer's face: start hitting even harder, to punish the witness of this ridiculous discomfiture? Resume questioning as if nothing had happened? Or else . . . It was the expression in the prisoner's eyes that astonished him: a perfect detachment, an almost smiling lucidity. The officer saw that the man thrown to the ground was staring at the tiny trace of blue through the window, that line of sky which he could manage to see from the floor.

He helped Volsky back onto the stool, and repeated his question, to which he had received only negative replies.

'I will ask again. Do you admit that you intended to fly the German aircraft exhibited at the so-called Blockade Museum and drop bombs on Smolny, in order to kill the members of the city's leadership?'

If Volsky had not previously heard tell of demented accusations of this type he would have thought he was going mad. But this forensic delirium was no longer a secret, people spoke of it, both terrified and almost elated by the excessiveness of the absurdity: such and such a person had been shot for attempting to poison the waters of all the great rivers in the country, another was said to have contrived to create a dozen subversive organizations in a village of a hundred inhabitants . . . And now here he was, planning to take off in an aircraft riddled with shrapnel which had had its undercarriage torn away!

He was silent. There was not much choice. Deny it and lay himself open to more blows? Agree and sign his own death warrant?

Suddenly the investigating officer's voice slid down into a whisper: 'Say you wanted to bomb Smolny to eliminate anti-Party factionalists at the heart of the city's leadership.' And Volsky saw he was already putting this crackpot confession into writing. The young officer was indeed engaged in fabricating a criminal, but a criminal inspired by a praiseworthy desire to struggle against the enemies of the Party and its Guide. Lowering his head slightly, Volsky could see through the basement window a little snow and the reflection of the sky in a window pane.

Every day in the camp he found a moment of freedom to meet Mila's gaze up in the sky.

The life of a prisoner did not destroy him. He had often had occasion to sleep on the ground at the front, in mud or under snow. Here the bedsteads in huts equipped with stoves could almost seem comfortable. Cutting down trees was painful work but his arms retained the knack of handling the weight of shells. Hunger and scurvy were killers and yet, compared with the hundred and twenty-five grams of bread during the blockade, the poorest food seemed lavish.

As for the length of his sentence, four and a half years in a camp, it was enough to make you smile: ten years of hard labour was the modest norm here. 'Praise be for that officer's nosebleed,' Volsky would say to himself.

And in the worst hours of despair there was this sky, whether grey, luminous or nocturnal, and the link created by the power of a single gaze, beyond the world of human beings.

The clemency of his own sentence made him hope for an even lighter penalty for Mila. What could she be accused of? Bringing a notebook stained with earth to the museum? Volsky contrived to believe her acquitted, free, settled with the children in their old *izba*: in the evening she would step outside under the quivering of the first stars, look up at the sky . . . Then this hope became muddied, he recalled that for a long time the repressions had parted company with all logic. He, who had never set foot in the cockpit of an aircraft, was said to have decided to bomb Leningrad. Even crazier intentions could have been attributed to Mila. She might have been sent to a camp thousands of miles from the one where he was!

This supposition was a hideous torment. And yet, on occasion, he ventured on a declaration whose harsh and beautiful truth he feared himself: nothing could alter the moment when their eyes rose up to encounter one another. Then he pictured Mila amid white fields, her face uplifted towards the slow swirling of the snow.

This vision helped him not to live in hatred, which was a good way of surviving in the camp. He understood this when one day in spring he found himself buried under a pile of tree trunks: a gigantic pyramid of cedar stems, which the prisoners were preparing to float downriver. The break up of the ice was happening early and more violently than usual. The stack of tree trunks stirred, shaken by the vibration of the ice floes, waking into life on that great Siberian river. And all at once the mountain of logs began rolling, scattering. The timber was swallowed into cavities in the ice shelf, hurtled into the water, rose up vertically, fell back, reared up into walls that caved in . . . Several prisoners were trapped by the collapse. Two or three vanished into the river. They were able to save one of them, whose shoulder was shattered.

Volsky remained pinned to the ground low down on the shore, close to the menacing procession of disintegrating ice floes. His chest crushed, his legs caught in the tangle of tree trunks, he could neither cry out nor move. When he regained consciousness night had fallen and he guessed that the search, if there had been one, had not been very thorough. A prisoner's life was worth nothing and nobody wanted to lose his own by venturing into a chaotic mass of logs that threatened to subside and slide into the river at any moment. They must have reckoned that he had drowned.

All that was left of his voice was a hissing whisper, all he could move was his hands, which explored his wooden tomb in the darkness. Through the criss-crossed tree trunks he could see a triangle of stars.

The pain reached what he thought would prove to be a fatal threshold, then it subsided, or rather he became used to this threshold. His thirst became more cruel than the pain and only let up during those moments when his gaze escaped between the wooden stems into the sky. Then his mind cleared and, as there was no longer anyone to convince, not even himself, the simplicity of what he understood was conclusive.

He understood that in all he had lived through the

only thing that was true was the sky, looked at on the same day, perhaps at the same moment, by two beings who loved one another. Everything else was more or less irrelevant. Among the prisoners he had met murderers without remorse and innocent people who spent their time reproaching themselves. Cowards, lapsed heroes, the suicidal. Sybarites sentenced to twenty years, who dreamed of meals a woman would cook for them when they left the camp. Gentle people, sadists, crooks, righters of wrongs. Thinkers, who perceived this place of labour and death as the result of a humanistic theory badly applied. An orthodox priest who averred that suffering was given by God so that man should expiate, better himself.

All of this seemed equally trifling to him now. And when he thought again about the world of free people, the difference between it and the miseries and joys of this place seemed minimal. If three tiny fragments of tea leaf chanced to fall into a prisoner's battered cup, he relished them. In Leningrad during the interval at the opera (he remembered *Rigoletto*) a woman sipped champagne with the same pleasure. Their sufferings were also comparable. Both the prisoner and the woman had painful shoes. Hers were narrow evening shoes which she took off during the performance. The prisoner suffered from what they wore in the camp, sections of tyres into which you thrust your foot wrapped in rags and fastened with string. The woman at the opera knew that somewhere in the world there were millions of beings transformed into gaunt animals, their faces blackened by the polar winds. But this did not stop her drinking her glass of wine amid the glittering of the great mirrors. The prisoner knew that a warm and brilliant life was lived elsewhere in tranquillity but this did not spoil his pleasure as he chewed those fragments of tea leaf . . .

At moments the pain grew sharper, only leaving him with a vague awareness: it was his thirst that made him picture that prisoner with his cup of tea, the woman imbibing her cold sparkling wine from a tall glass. So, it was all even less significant.

The water was close, a powerful current just beside his crushed body, and also ice, in little stalactites beneath the tree trunks. He reached out his hand, the effort increased the pain, he lost consciousness.

At the beginning of the second day the snow began to swirl around in great lazy flakes. Volsky felt the coolness of the crystals on his parched lips. And once more pictured a field in winter, a woman looking up into a white flurry.

He knew he had few hours to live and the conciseness of his thinking seemed to take account of this limited time. The words of the priest came back to him: the sufferings God inflicts so that man may expiate, purify himself . . . The smile this brought cracked his dried lips. If that were the case, so many men should be infinitely pure. In the camp. In the country ravaged by war. And, indeed, by the purges! After everything these people had endured they should have been as shining as saints! And yet, after ten years of suffering, a prisoner could still kill for an extra slice of bread. God . . . Volsky remembered the buckles on the shoulder belts worn by the German soldiers. '*Gott mit uns*,' God is with us, was embossed on the metal. These soldiers had also suffered. So . . .

He looked up: night was beginning to fall and in the tangle of tree trunks above his head there shone a pale, ashen cluster of stars. A woman saw it, at that moment, and knew that he, too, was looking at the sky . . . He grasped that even God no longer had any importance from the moment when those two pairs of eyes existed. Or, at least, not this god of human beings, this lover of suffering and belts.

The thirst torturing him became something else – the burning desire to tell the woman that nothing had any meaning without these moments looking at the sky.

In the night, or else it was the darkness of his lost consciousness, he heard a very faint voice: somebody was singing but occasionally forgetting the words, and so had to be prompted.

They had found Volsky thanks to these few snatches of song, explained the men who had heard him. Engineers, who had come with their explosives to blow up the fortress wall of tree trunks soldered together by the ice.

The singing that had welled up within him became another life, unconnected to the passing of the days. The world's bustle seemed to him even more feverish and devoid of sense. From his bed in the camp's sick bay he could see the ice floes hurtling along, revolving and disintegrating in the river. Daylight and darkness rushed by, speeded up. The prisoners assembled for roll call, went off to work, returned. And even when the guards, on a whim, made them wait for long hours in the rain, this torment expressed nothing more than a ludicrous eagerness to do harm, to demonstrate their power as petty torturers. He soon found himself back in the ranks, upright on legs covered in bruises. In the old days his anger would have flared up at the guards' gratuitous cruelty. Now all he perceived was a vortex of wills, desires, base deeds. He thirsted to tell these men what he had understood in his tomb of timber and ice, and this urge remained intact. But the necessary words belonged to a language he had never yet spoken. Hidden among the ranks of the prisoners who cursed their tormentors, he would raise his eyes and slip away into the life he had imagined.

*　　*　　*

212

When he was released it seemed to make no difference to this other life. The lorry taking him drove out through the entrance ('Forward to the Victory of Communist Labour!' was inscribed above the iron gates) and the camp vanished behind a hill turned russet by the autumn. 'Just a twist of the steering wheel,' thought Volsky, 'and a whole planet is swept away, like a fragment of ice in a river.' A terrifying planet of misery, cruelty, hope, prayers and suddenly, nothing: a road gleaming with rain, this sparse northern vegetation, waiting for winter.

He dwelt in a world where it was all one to him. Found work at a marshalling yard, lodged nearby, in a room whose windows looked out on the tracks. People saw him as halfway between a not-very-bright worker and an ex-prisoner eager for his past to be forgotten. Sometimes they must even have thought him a bit soft in the head. He would be observed, alone, among the snow-dusted tracks, his head thrown back, scanning a perfectly empty sky with half-closed eyes.

After months of research, Volsky learned that Mila had been given a sentence, that she was serving somewhere in a camp. But where? And what sentence? 'Ten years of hard labour,' replied a former employee at the Blockade Museum, with whom he had managed to establish contact. Ten years. He did the sums, saw opening up within him an abyss of five years' wait, was not plunged into despair. He knew that every day Mila's gaze joined him in the increasingly wintry sky and that at such moments time did not exist.

213

Twenty or thirty years later Volsky would read accounts written by former prisoners. Some spoke of how their lives were destroyed, others told how they managed to resume 'normal life'. He would then reflect that, whilst his own life had remained intact, it was the world that, little by little, faded away.

He did not have to wait five years. Two and a half years later Stalin died and in the human tide pouring out through the gates of the camps Volsky was sure he would find Mila again.

One evening in April he was walking beside the railway track on his return from work and from a long way off saw a woman seated on a little bench beneath the windows of the building where he lived. He slowed his pace, hearing dull, heavy drumbeats pounding in his brain. The woman's hair was white and her face, seen in profile, lined with deep wrinkles. 'More than seven years in a camp . . .' he thought and felt himself bowed down beneath a weight pressing him towards the earth. Mila's face, aged, was a final ordeal for him, possibly the hardest. And yet this culminating blow, struck by a god who delights in causing suffering, seemed to him petty and futile. Nothing could harm a life that would be reborn beneath the sky where for so many years their eyes had met.

His urge to say this was so acute that he broke into a run.

The woman looked round. It was not Mila! A much older woman, who had been arrested with her, who had promised Mila she would find him. What she had to say amounted to a few words. 'Ten years in a camp without the right to correspondence,' such was the official sentence. Few people knew that this 'without the right to correspondence' signified that the condemned person was shot following the verdict. Sometimes letters from family members continued to arrive throughout those ten years of waiting . . .

Volsky remained sitting down, his eyes fixed upon the silhouette of the woman as she walked away, jolting from one sleeper to the next. He should have detained this freed prisoner, asked her questions, offered her tea, given her shelter . . . He would have done so but the world, already scarcely real, had vanished. There was nothing but these rails disappearing into the dusk, this elderly woman, walking away into the void, the words she had spoken, the last words that concerned him. An empty world.

He got up, looked at the sky. And sensed on his lips the emergence of a voice that would reach Mila. His lungs dilated. But instead of a cry, what came out was a long whisper tormented by a thirst. A terrible craving. One that came from not knowing how, with words, to bring the one he loved back to life.

V

'The same thirst . . .' thinks Shutov as he watches the old man taking long draughts of cold tea.

'Forgive me, I've grown unused to talking.' Volsky smiles, sets the cup down on the bedside table again. They are silent, not knowing how to conclude this nocturnal recital. To say goodbye, part, go to bed? Shutov understands that he has just entered a world where one cannot lie, not by word or gesture. He stares into the blackness outside the window: a brief period of dark at the heart of a northern summer night. On the silent television screen the procession of heads of state can be seen entering a banqueting hall . . .

The old man has been speaking for barely an hour. His youth, the dead city in the blockade, the war, the camp. And the wild cherry blossom fluttering down on a spring evening long ago.

His account has been restricted by a fear of relating facts too familiar, of repeating himself. On several occasions he has observed: 'All this is well known now.' It was as if he were afraid of placing his own story beside the epic narratives that have exhausted the subject. 'Not everyone had my luck, you know.' Not everyone, no, those who died of hunger during the blockade, those

219

who were killed in battle, those who froze to death in the ice of the camps.

Shutov looks away, the words he could utter seem so pointless. On the screen an aerial view of London, a documentary about the new Russian elite, the title: *Moscow on Thames* . . .

'There's nothing exceptional about my case,' the old man had also remarked. Shutov thinks about this: it is true, even in his youth he heard tell of these broken lives. Millions of souls lacerated by the barbed wire. The camps occupied a twentieth of the vast expanse of the Soviet Union, ten times the area of Great Britain, whose green pastures are just now gliding past on the screen. To disappear into this void was not a rare fate, old Volsky is right.

A voice within Shutov rebels: but no, the life story that has just been confided to him is unique and incomparable . . . He pictures a woman amid the huts surrounded by watchtowers and a man in a line of prisoners. They both look up, observe the slow-moving clouds, feel the cold kiss of snowflakes on their brows. They are thousands of miles apart. And very close to one another, as close as the mist from their breathing.

Shutov knows what he should ask Volsky now: after that, did he ever again seek to meet up in the sky with the eyes of the one he loved?

He hesitates, stammers: 'And after that . . . ?' As if he wanted to know how the story ended, as if the presence of the old man in this little room were not already an ending.

Volsky takes another drink, then, in a voice much

less tense, murmurs: 'Afterwards . . . I hardly spoke any more and people began to believe I was dumb. It was as if I were dead, or at least absent from their world.'

This absence was made up of frozen dusks in a small Siberian town, the place where his life had run aground. Of work which reminded him of his labour as a prisoner. Of alcohol, the only means of escape for him, as for so many others. He remained silent, knowing now that one could live very well without words and that all people needed was his strength, his resignation, yes, precisely that, his absence.

There was only one day when he broke his silence. He was working in a machine shop where they repaired the side panels of coaches, the foreman swore at him, called him a filthy jailbird. Volsky hit out and muttered at the man, as he lay there on the ground: 'Choose your weapons, sir!'

The officer in the militia who interrogated him was young, very self-assured. Volsky noticed at once that he resembled the investigating officer who had sent him to the camp. The same fair hair, the same uniform too big for a puny body. There was also a little low window that looked out onto a snowy street . . .

Volsky stopped answering, dazzled by a truth that suddenly threw light on this world whose obtuse cruelty he had sought to understand. So this was it: a perpetual vortex, a circle dance with recurring roles, similar faces, always parallel circumstances. And always the same will to deny that which is truest, most profound in man. Snow, a woman looking up at the sky . . .

'According to the foreman,' the officer was saying, 'you made anti-Soviet statements while causing him bodily harm . . .'

Staring at this young face, animated by fierce scowls, Volsky smiled and remained silent. The world that had just revealed its insane governing principle no longer interested him. 'A mad merry-go-round,' he thought. 'The same faces, the same wooden animals revolving faster and faster.' A few years after the war with its millions of dead they were already testing a new bomb (he had read about it in a newspaper) which would be able to kill even more people. Three years after Stalin's death they were explaining that everyone he had massacred had been annihilated by mistake, thanks to a simple doctrinal distortion. And now there was this little blond officer, getting heated, yelling, thumping his fist on the table, no doubt about to strike the prisoner sitting in front of him. 'And then this blond fellow's nose will start bleeding. And I'll advise him to pick up a handful of snow. He'll do this. And we'll have a brief, humane interlude . . .'

Volsky realized he had been saying all this aloud and the officer was listening to him, open-mouthed and wide-eyed. 'You'll see. A handful of snow and the bleeding will stop . . .' He was then overtaken by a violent outburst of laughter, almost painful, for his wrists, tied behind his back, wrenched his shoulder at each guffaw. 'It's a nightmare circus! A great nightmare circus!' he exclaimed, amazed to find this simple phrase summed up the madness of the world so well.

He spent a little less than a year in a mental home. As he was silent, the staff regarded him as a good patient, a shadow, an absence. Despite its wretched, dilapidated state, the place did not seem sinister to him. And the patients there merely echoed the fevers and obsessions of the outside world, as if in a strange mental magnifying glass. One man, so thin his face was almost blue, spent his time hiding behind the screen of his raised hands, a droll shield to protect him against the torturers coming from his past. Others converted their beds into snail shells which they rarely left, their heads hunched between their shoulders. A former theatre director was perpetually accusing and defending himself, playing the roles both of investigating magistrate and prisoner. One old man spent his days observing the glistening drops of water falling from the roof when the ice melted. His face was radiant. There was also a man in perfect mental health, an elderly Lithuanian with whom Volsky made friends. This man had chosen to take refuge here to escape from the purges. He told the story of his life very calmly, described the places where he had lived. But whenever Volsky tried to explain to him that Stalin was dead and it was now possible to leave the asylum the Lithuanian became suspicious and asked him in a hoarse voice: 'Why are you lying to me? I know perfectly well he will never die!'

Madmen, yes, Volsky said to himself. Then thought back to what he had lived through during the blockade, in the war and in the camp. And the madness of the patients seemed a good deal more reasonable than the society which had locked them up.

The doctor in charge of the annual inspection turned out to be a native of Leningrad. Volsky talked with him for a long time: a whole litany of streets, canals, theatres, memories of a city which neither of them had seen for years. 'Hold on to something concrete,' he advised Volsky, as he signed the authorization for his discharge. 'But above all, think up a project, a dream. Dream of returning to Leningrad one day, for example.'

He followed the doctor's advice, after a fashion. According to the laws of the time, an ex-prisoner's place of residence had to be at least sixty miles from any of the big cities. Volsky settled in a small town to the north of Leningrad, not far, he told himself, from the former battlefields.

The little town welcomed him with a noise of engines: a car stuck in a quagmire, a length of cable, a tractor attempting to rescue some people shipwrecked in the mud. Volsky gathered up an armful of branches from the roadside, threw them under the wheels of the car. 'Something concrete,' he thought as he went on his way, 'a fine project for a madman who's just been let out.'

Two days later in the same street Volsky wept. A line of children was proceeding along this muddy highway;

224

he stopped and suddenly realized what kind of children they were. During those years after Stalin's massacres and the bloodbath of the war, orphans were too numerous to cause any surprise. But the orphans he was seeing ought not to have shown themselves: these were the rejects, for the most part carefully hidden from view. Disabled, mentally ill, blind . . . crushed by the war or else brought into the world in a hut in one of the camps. Too weak to be sent to a re-education colony, too damaged to be moulded into good little workers in an ordinary orphanage.

The line walked slowly, making halting progress. The children clung to one another, some of them fell, the accompanying adult picked them up the way you lift a sack. The damp snow must have made impracticable the route they usually took, where they would remain unseen. So they had to be brought along the little town's main street . . . Already they were disappearing into the grey winter dusk. At the very end Volsky saw a little girl with a heavy limp, sinking down at each step of her misshapen leg, straightening herself up with an abrupt jerk. It was on seeing her that he bit his lip to hold back his tears.

He discovered their orphanage the same evening, an old building made of almost black bricks, divided into rooms by plywood partitions, part dormitories, part communal rooms. 'Much like in our huts at the camp,' thought Volsky.

The next day he returned, offered his services. As teacher or supervisor? He did not know what kind of training these children were given. He was engaged at once, for indeed they were given nothing. The children were temporarily parked here. The weakest died. Others, considered to be mentally ill, were waiting to be sent to an adult mental home.

It was pointless to be indignant, to make demands: the staff consisted of two elderly women and a single supervisor, a man with the stump of an arm lost in the war. The director, a self-effacing little woman, explained in embarrassed tones: 'It's hard to know who's looking after whom: us after the children or the children after us . . .'

The first day, when he came into the main hall where all the children were assembled, Volsky studied them discreetly, attempting to see each face, each figure, as unique. And suddenly, acting on impulse, began humming, softly at first, just a little murmur, then in tones which rose above the noise, the weeping. A hesitant litany responded to him, their heads began to move with the rhythm, their bodies to sway gently. A little girl, her face marked by the long gash of a scar, came up and offered him a fragment of red glass, her treasure, no doubt.

He gave them all that he had – his voice. Began to teach them a little singing, tunes easy to remember, melodies whose rhythms infused new life into these frail bodies paralyzed by illness and injuries. The lines of the songs had to be noted down and, without being aware of it, the children wrote out their first words, managed their first reading. Textbooks did not exist and Volsky was feeling his way in the art of teaching,

226

so new to him. The idea occurred of getting them to imagine through gesture and facial expression the story told by a song: a horseman arriving beneath the windows of the house where he was born, the welcome given him by his mother and his beloved . . . These children, condemned to a life as shadows, thus began to gain access to a life where changing your destiny was possible, where they were listened to, loved. Where they offered love.

He himself learned a great deal during those first months. Among the thirty or so children living at the orphanage there were faces that reminded him of Mila's children. A boy with red hair, who had a fine resonant voice, was a little like Mandarin, though without his energy and ebullience. The parallel was distressing and yet this was how Volsky contrived to conquer the world's whirligig absurdity. Yes, one could resist its bleak logic. As this redhead did just now, standing in front of the others and singing about a horseman riding through a snowstorm.

The songs spoke of 'the wide blue sea' and Volsky told them what he knew of seas and oceans. One of the ballads featured a boyar and, as a makeshift history teacher, he acted out scenes from the Russian past for his pupils, now as a prince, now as a serf.

He told them about the three musketeers as well, mimed battles and cavalcades, imitated the swish of a sword slicing through the air, fluttered a folded newspaper – a fan for a fair lady seated at a castle window . . . For the children this was their first journey abroad, an inconceivable thing within that country barricaded behind its iron curtain.

One evening he sang d'Artagnan's song . . .

From that day forward an idea took hold of him: to get these orphans to perform in a play, whatever their disability might be. He allocated roles and, remembering all the extra walk-on actors in the performances staged during the blockade, invented characters and wrote little scenes so that everyone should have their couple of lines to say or sing.

The show he planned to stage often differed greatly from that old operetta. Their voices were weak; they soon ran out of breath. Some of the children had difficulty moving. The costumes, sewn by the women at the orphanage using old scraps of material, lacked theatrical brio. But the ingenuity of these little actors transfigured everything. A fragment of glass enmeshed in wire became a jewelled crown; battered old boots, with cardboard added to them, were transformed into thigh boots . . . Acting helped the children to forget their own bodies. The little girl Volsky had seen limping on the muddy road took the part of Marie and instinctively concealed her gait by skipping mischievously from one pose to another.

After dozens of rehearsals he perceived the real meaning of what had at first seemed like an amusing game. On stage his pupils forgot their suffering. But above all, they were leading a life that no one could forbid them. In a few minutes of acting each of them escaped from the world that had condemned them to non-existence.

Their first audience consisted of five people: the two women on the staff, the supervisor, the director and Volsky. At one of the subsequent performances the driver who delivered coal once a month joined them. Then an assistant from a nearby bakery. A few people who lived in the locality and their friends . . . Some came in search of entertainment, something in short supply in that bleak little town. In others one could sense curiosity about an unusual novelty: that bunch of sick kids were putting on a show!

One day in May the play was performed in front of a very different audience. The director had told Volsky in tremulous tones the previous day that they had been 'denounced', that there was talk in the town of an underground theatre and the Party Committee was going to send an inspection. Observing her face twitching with fear, Volsky reflected that the three years that had passed since Stalin's death were nothing, it might perhaps take thirty years for her features to relax, for the woman no longer to tremble at every word.

The Party inspector marched into the hall and stood like a ponderous monolith at its centre. A huge body hewn from a single block, a broad slab of a face, a voice trained to give orders. 'Begin!' she said to Volsky, without so much as greeting him and, with a movement of her chin, she indicated to her retinue, two women and a

229

man, that they should seat themselves in the front row.

'The same merry-go-round,' thought Volsky, 'the same faces turning up and manifesting more of the world's gratuitous cruelty. This one has the face of a watchdog, just like that other inspector, in the old days, who came into Mila's lesson . . .' It was not so much the recurrence of it that surprised him: he knew the workings of this absurd law. It was the deliberately contrived ugliness of the visitation, yes, the wilful contrivance of evil.

The woman peered at the stage with a contemptuous sneer, dilating her nostrils from time to time, as if these costumed children smelled bad. They acted particularly well, as it happened, sensing that this was a special performance. 'What's she going to accuse me of?' Volsky wondered, occasionally noting the faces the inspector was pulling. 'A play not conforming to ideological precepts? Absence of educational significance? Lack of class consciousness?' He was not uneasy, realizing that the children would not know such a verdict was foreseeable. He had arranged for the supervisor to take them out for a walk as soon as it ended. Later they could be told that their acting had been much appreciated but from now on they would have to learn different songs . . .

He had pictured the sequence of events along the lines of what used to happen under Stalin. From the judges: monolithic silence, verdict, punishment. But times had changed, they improvised now, they innovated . . .

Suddenly the woman waved her arms with a shout that made the whole company jump: 'Stop this circus! Enough! Not only do you have these children

230

performing foolish antics, totally alien to our class consciousness, but . . . but . . .'

The children broke off their performance, the adults on their feet surrounding the inspector were waiting in awe for the final phase of the eruption. 'But . . . but . . .' She was visibly searching for a more aesthetic argument to prop up her accusation.

'But . . . you haven't even taught your pupils how to move properly on stage. They're all walking like wooden marionettes! That one, that boy, especially. The musketeer, if you can call him that. Is he sleepwalking or what? You could have shown him the proper way for a soldier to march!'

She turned to Volsky. Silence fell. On the stage the red-haired boy who played d'Artagnan was standing very straight, his gaze far away above the heads of his comrades.

'That child isn't sleepwalking, Comrade Inspector. He's . . . blind.'

Everyone froze. Volsky was about to say more, then changed his mind. Impossible to describe the months of rehearsal during which the redhead, with obstinate patience, had learned to conquer the darkness on the stage. Step by step, the youth had learned the positions of each actor, the place each line was directed to, had mastered the play for himself like a moving picture that was alive within him. Few were the spectators who noticed his blindness. Generally people had the impression that he could see his little Marie very well as she emerged through a great cardboard gateway and rushed towards him.

231

The inspector blew her nose noisily on a square of striped fabric, coughed, blew her nose again, muttered, 'I'll come back . . .' and left the hall.

Volsky signalled to the children, the play continued . . . Songs, the clash of wooden swords, painted blue for lack of silver paint, the flickering flame of a candle on the table where Marie was writing a letter. The inspector entered silently, sat on a chair near the door.

'To you, my beloved, I shall confide my dream . . .' the red-haired boy was singing.

During his long life Volsky would come to know dozens of orphanages, hospitals, re-education colonies. He taught singing and movement to those who were afraid to speak and whose bodies only had memories of violent brutality: abandoned and disabled children, young delinquents. Above all, he taught them how to exist otherwise than in the world manufactured by the petty cruelty of men . . . One of his first pupils, the red-haired boy, would tell him one day that when he sang d'Artagnan's song, about 'the sky where the stars float above' he could see the clusters of stars, he understood how they might look.

Volsky had acted as Mila had asked him to on the day of their arrest: tried to live without looking back at their past, got married, had a son. Clear-headed, he considered that this life was close enough to happiness and forbade himself to wish for more. Routine allowed him not to make comparisons between this existence and what he had known with Mila.

During the post-Stalin thaw his work made him almost famous for a time: the newspapers spoke of his 'innovative educational methods', there was even a book about him. He was offered a post in a research institute. He refused it, continuing to choose out-of-the-way places, establishments where he felt truly useful. His wanderings finally wearied his wife, they divorced. His son, when he reached adulthood, also moved away and much later Volsky learned that he had gone to live in Germany . . .

At the time of the collapse of the USSR Volsky was working in Central Asia and already used a wheelchair to get about. 'Once a whole forest fell on top of me,' he would say jokingly to doctors, explaining how, when he was still young, he had found himself crushed beneath a pyramid of cedar trunks. He did not specify that this had occurred in a camp. For new generations such things belonged to a legendary past . . . Like the archives from the time of the purges, which were now being opened up and which Volsky could consult in Moscow. The legal file on Mila was there, the now yellow pages from the interrogations she had undergone. From reading these depositions he learned that she had done everything possible to exculpate him, taking on herself the accusations levelled at them both. 'So what saved me wasn't that little officer's nosebleed . . .' he thought, and this sacrifice, which had saved his life, reminded him again that the evil of this world could be put to rout by the will of a single human being.

A year later one of his former pupils helped him to

return to Leningrad, found him this little room in a communal flat.

Volsky did not feel unhappy, just a little overtaken by the speed of the changes.

One day his neighbours informed him that a big move was being planned, a complicated exchange which would allow each of them to have a self-contained one-room flat in the suburbs. He did not grasp all the details of the scheme. Quite simply he now saw smartly dressed men coming in and out, talking about square metres and works to be undertaken, calculating in dollars. A blonde woman often appeared among them, talking about makes of tiles, baths, furniture. The men called her Yana. Volsky liked hearing her voice. He even thought that some day he might be able to tell her his life story . . .

Then one evening he heard a conversation outside the door of his room. Yana and several men were having a somewhat heated discussion about a move which was taking a long time to happen. Suddenly Volsky grasped that they were talking about him. 'Listen, be realistic,' Yana was saying, evidently trying to calm things down. 'The old man's here. There's nothing to be done about it. Obviously it would suit us if he departed this vale of tears in the meantime, but let's not be too optimistic. He may be deaf and bedridden, but he could live to be a hundred. What I'm proposing is a very reasonable solution . . .'

Volsky stopped listening and from that day forward

no longer replied when spoken to. They took him now for a deaf-mute. He noticed that this made no great difference to his relationship with the people bustling around the flat. Their attitude may even have become less hypocritical.

And Shutov remembers now. He has heard the name 'Volsky' in his youth. Thirty years ago. Articles speaking of a teacher who used drama to bring new life to handicapped children and young tearaways. For journalists in the days of censorship such topics offered a rare zone of freedom: a unique individual who refuses honours and a good career is already in discreet revolt against the massive concrete structure of the regime.

The old man drinks his cold tea. The television, with the sound switched off, shows videos of blonde girls and young black men swaying their hips with expressions ranging from the arrogant to the lascivious. Night-time TV. The light of a lamp fixed to the back of the bed, a dark window, this almost empty room. In a few hours the paramedics will come to take the old man away. So it really is the end of this nocturnal recital.

Shutov is still eager to know what became of the sky where two loving gazes used to meet, during those long years. But it is too late to ask, Volsky's life has merged into that of the country's battered past: wars, camps, the utter fragility of any bond between two human beings. A heroic life, a life sacrificed. A life Shutov might himself have encountered, since he spent his own childhood in an orphanage. 'Yes, I could have had Volsky as my singing teacher,' he thinks.

'You know, I've got nothing against your friend, Yana,' says the old man, putting his cup down on the night table. 'Nor the others, either. Their life isn't at all enviable. Imagine, they have to own all this!'

He makes a broad gesture and Shutov sees clearly that 'all this' is Yana's new apartment but also the vast television screen and the documentary about the Russian elite settling in London, their town houses, their country residences and the cocktail party where at this moment they are all meeting, and this wholly new way of life which Shutov simply cannot comprehend.

'When it comes down to it, we had such an easy life!' says the old man. 'We had no possessions and yet we knew we were happy. In the space between two bullets whistling past, as you might say . . .' He smiles and adds in jesting tones: 'No, but look at those poor people. They're not happy!' A reception can be seen at a luxury hotel in London, the tense smiles of the women, the glistening faces of the men. 'We used to pull faces like that at the Conservatoire when they made us listen to cantatas glorifying Stalin . . .' He laughs softly and his hand makes the same gesture again: 'All this.' Very physically, Shutov feels that the world thus referred to is one that spreads itself out horizontally, flat and perfectly level in each of its components. Yes, a flattened world.

'If you could switch off now . . .' asks Volsky. Shutov seizes the remote control, gets confused (on the screen an old tram appears, slipping along silently, disappearing up a street), finally succeeds in switching off.

Volsky's face resumes the same expression as at the start of the night: calm, detached, perhaps even a little distant. Shutov does not expect any further word from him. It has all been said, all that remains to be done is to bid him goodnight and take a few hours' sleep before Vlad and the paramedics arrive.

The voice that rings out is strikingly firm.

'I have never ceased meeting her gaze. Even when I learned that she was dead . . . And nobody could forbid me to believe that she saw me too. And tonight I know she is still looking up at the sky. And nobody, you understand, nobody will dare to deny it!'

The voice is so forceful that Shutov stands up. It is the voice of a former singer or perhaps an artillery officer calling out orders amid explosions. Shutov sits down again, ventures a brief gesture, on the point of speaking, but remains silent. Volsky's features relax, his eyelids close lightly. His hands rest motionless alongside his body. Shutov realizes that it was not the determined voice that had brought him to his feet. The old man's words had summoned up a lofty radiance in this flattened world, one which seemed to raise the ceiling of that little room.

In a very much fainter echo of that cry comes a whisper of regret, which Volsky keeps more or less to himself: 'A shame, though, not to have seen the Lukhta again . . . The shore where we gave our last concert . . . The trees I planted with Mila . . . You go to sleep. Don't worry . . . I can manage very well on my own . . .'

He grasps the switch on the lamp above his bed. Shutov stands up, goes to the door. He takes slow steps, looking as if he were trying to delay his departure, to come up with some last word that he had to say and which he had forgotten.

'Wait, just a moment!' he finally blurts out and rushes into Vlad's office. Beside the telephone, the list of useful numbers the young man had left for him when he went out: ambulance, police, taxi . . . Shutov makes a call, orders a taxi, comes running back into Volsky's bedroom, gets his words in a tangle, apologizes, explains his plan to him. The old man smiles: 'I'm partial to adventures, but I shall need to put on my glad rags. There, on the hook, behind the door, a windcheater and trousers . . .'

Shutov asks the taxi driver to come up and help him carry 'an invalid' downstairs, he says, keeping things simple. At once the powerfully built, stocky young man begins to express his displeasure. When he learns that this will not be a simple trip to a hospital but a long drive outside the city he goes off the deep end: 'No chance! I don't do tourist trips. You should have booked a minibus, mate . . .' Shutov insists, clumsily, realizing that current parlance has changed, as well as every-thing else, and that his arguments (an old soldier who wants to revisit the places where he fought in the war) must seem surreal.

'Look, mate, there's no set fare for trips like that. And what's more it's the middle of the night . . .' The driver turns towards the door to show he is about to go. Shutov hates this thick neck, this very round skull with its close-cropped hair, the sullen look of someone who knows the other man is no match for him.

'I'll pay what it costs. Tell me your price. We can agree on a figure.'

'But I'm telling you there's no fixed fare. And we've got to lug the . . . grandpa downstairs into the bargain!'

'A hundred dollars, would that do?'

'You're joking. For a trip like that . . .'

'Five hundred?'

'Look, mate, you have a think about it and call me next week. Okay?'

He turns away, opens the door. Shutov catches him on the landing, negotiates, ends up giving him three hundred-dollar notes. He glimpses a rather childish delight on the man's face: pleasure at having ripped off a simpleton, surprise, pride in having come out on top. Money does not yet have an established value in this new country, there's an element of roulette about it and he has won.

He drives quite slowly at first, doubtless for fear of running into a police patrol. But once outside the city, he speeds along, straight over every crossroads. It feels as if he is beginning to relish this escapade. Shutov winds down the window: monotonous suburban streets hurtle past, a city asleep, and from time to time, within the endless slabs of building fronts, a window lit up, very yellow, a life keeping watch.

At last, like the lash of a branch, the scent of grass, the bitter night smell of foliage. The car leaves the main road, begins jolting along badly paved lanes. Two or three times the old man tries to point the way but the driver rejoins: 'No, mate. That village doesn't exist any more . . . You see, there's a shopping centre there

240

now . . .' His tone of voice has changed, he responds to Volsky in somewhat contrite tones . . .

And suddenly he brakes, surprised himself by a barrier across the road.

Beyond it rises a veritable wall, at least twelve feet high. A bronze plaque set into a stone pillar gleams in the headlights. Richly ornamental letters imitating gothic script: '*Palatine Residential Estate: Private Road. Residents only.*' The driver gets out, with Shutov close behind him. Beyond a monumental wrought-iron gate can be seen the outlines of the 'palaces', illuminated by the floodlights of a building site. A crane throws the shadow of its hook across a wall. A bulldozer sleeps beneath a tree. Site offices stationed at each corner of the enclosure are reminiscent of watchtowers . . .

The resemblance is not lost on Volsky. 'It looks like a prison,' he murmurs, when the two men get back into the car.

'What do you want to do?' asks the driver. 'Try and work our way round it?' And without waiting for a word from Shutov and Volsky he drives off. Rising to this challenge becomes a point of honour for him. The car gets stuck in the mud almost at once and Shutov has the door half open, ready to get out and push. 'It's okay!' snorts the driver, twisting the wheel and looking as if he were wrestling a bull with his bare hands. A long hysterical scream from the engine, a painful slithering and finally they shoot away, like a bat out of hell.

Their progress becomes steadier now, lulled as they sway broadly along an earth road, the rustling of tall plants can be heard against the sides of the car. The air smells more and more of the coolness of a river. The beam from the headlights comes up against a plantation of willows. They follow a slope. They stop. The headlights are switched off, their eyes quickly grow accustomed to the pale northern night. Silence settles and the ear begins to identify the tiniest rustlings. The music of the long willow leaves, the soporific purling of the current, from time to time a quick, frail call emitted by a bird in flight . . .

The driver helps Shutov to settle Volsky down at the shore's edge on the broad trunk of a felled tree whose timber, stripped of its bark, traces a white line in the darkness. Without needing to confer, the two men move away.

They inhale deeply, amazed by the lively sharpness of the air, by this calm found very close, after all, to the bustle of the festive city. To their right, against the background of the sky's ashen pallor, can be seen the line of the Palatine Residential Estate's enclosure ('Excelsior', 'Trianon' . . . Shutov remembers). On the far bank, coppices separated by long pathways can be divined. 'The trees Volsky and Mila planted,' he thinks, 'the graveyard . . .' In the sky a mass of transparent clouds; from time to time a star shivers, very close, alive.

The driver, sitting on a tree stump, mutters something. He turns his wrist to make out the illuminated dial of his watch in the darkness. Shutov reassures him: 'We'll be on our way soon . . .' 'No, let the old man take his time! I don't get much work at night . . .' His tone is still marked by a trace of guilt. 'He was really in the war here?' he asks. Shutov whispers, as if someone could hear them. Yes, it was here. The blockade of Leningrad; the last concert given by a theatre troupe; and then this old man, a young soldier at that time, pushing a gun along a frozen shore; Berlin. He becomes aware that he is now the only person in the world who knows Volsky's story so well . . .

He breaks off as he hears a voice rising up from the stream. The singing must have begun to ring out a moment ago but was mingled with the rustle of the willows, the murmur of the grasses. Now its melody dominates the silence, ripples effortlessly, like a very long, deep sigh. The driver is the first to get up, his face turned towards the source of the sound. Shutov stands as well, takes several steps towards the bank, stops. It is a song that gives back a forgotten, primal meaning to all that he can see: the earth, laden with dead, and yet so light, so full of springtime life, the ruins of an old *izba*, the imagined radiance of those who lived there and loved one another beneath its roof . . . And this sky, beginning to turn pale, which Shutov will never look at again the way he did before.

The return journey seems like lightning, almost instantaneous. As if these early-morning streets, totally empty, are vanishing as they pass through them.

And in the apartment this speeding up is even more feverish. The old man is hardly settled in his bed when Vlad arrives, passing the taxi driver in the hall. The door slams behind the latter, Shutov turns and sees placed there within the marble hand, 'Slava's hand', which lies on the occasional table, three hundred-dollar notes . . .

And already the paramedics are ringing the bell and cluttering up the corridor with their wheelchair. Shutov slips into Volsky's room hoping to be able to speak to him again, to tell him that his story . . . They shake hands. The paramedics are there, Vlad as well, they are busy packing the old man's books into a bag . . . Volsky's eyes smile at Shutov for the last time, then his face freezes into a final, indifferent mask.

The entrance hall teems with Vlad's friends, who are coming to the party at Yana's country house. The workmen make way for the two paramedics taking the old man away and start bringing in pipes for the plumbing. A housekeeper drags in a vacuum cleaner, dives into the little bedroom, now finally vacated. Various mobile phones ring, conversations overlap, become mixed up . . .

Shutov drinks a cup of tea in the kitchen and tries to picture himself as still involved in the whirlwind occurring all around him. 'Ma has just called,' shouts Vlad. 'She'll be here in ten minutes. She says hello . . .' Someone has switched on the television. 'To be on time, when every second counts . . .' 'You wouldn't have a cigarette?' a very young woman asks him and he suddenly feels struck dumb, stammers, gesticulates. She laughs, goes away.

It comes to him at last, with blinding clarity: he would never be able to exist in this new life.

Five minutes suffice to gather up his belongings, to

slip towards the door without being intercepted by Vlad, to leave . . .

At the airport he easily exchanges his ticket. 'The people who flew in for the celebrations are still here,' he is told. 'The ones who chose not to come, on account of the celebrations, will be flying in tomorrow . . .' So he has come at the right moment, at a dead time, so to speak.

In the plane he feels for the first time in his life as if he were going from nowhere to nowhere, or rather travelling without any real destination. And yet he has never felt his attachment to a native land more intensely. Except that the country in question is not a territory but an era; Volsky's. That monstrous Soviet era, the only period Shutov has lived through in Russia. Yes, monstrous, murderous, shamed and one during which, every day, a man looked up at the sky.

On his return home he finds a letter from Léa, words that seem to be addressed to someone other than himself. She thanks him, tells him he can keep the two piles of books as she no longer needs them and, for some reason, quotes Chekhov: in a short story one must cut the ending, which generally makes it too long. He realizes how much his abortive journey has changed him: he no longer comprehends these marks on paper in elegant feminine handwriting. Or rather he no longer comprehends the reasons for writing so many empty or false or hollow words. He can still manage to decode the little psychological games that lurk behind these sentences. An expression of thanks: Léa seeks to defuse the rancour of the man she has left. The books: a sentimental talisman, since she believes him to be a sentimental old man. The quotation from Chekhov: yes, let's make a clean break and avoid any follow-up.

All this can still be deciphered. But the life these words speak of is not worth the ink they are written in. It belongs only in the novels Léa has left behind in a corner of the room, little containers for verbal matter with no substance. 'Pygmyism,' he used to call it. Yes, his existence in this dovecote was a game for dolls, one of those little novels that, year in year out, recount the

246

miniature dramas of rather cynical, rather tedious ladies and gentlemen.

He now knows that the only words worth writing down arise when language is impossible. As in the case of that man and woman separated by thousands of miles of ice, whose eyes met under lightly falling snow. As with that red-haired boy, standing there transfixed, his blind eyes turned towards the stars he has never seen.

During the first few days following his trip, Shutov discovers, moment by moment, what absolutely must be told. Volsky, of course, but also that winter's evening in a café, the Café de la Gare, the loneliness of an old man murmuring in a void.

On arrival he had retrieved a parcel from his letter box: a book whose title was known to him. *After Her Life*. He remembered that woman walking along a narrow corridor, removing her make-up with a tissue, looking as if she were wiping away tears.

After her life. 'It's what I shall live from now on,' he tells himself.

He has a surprise, too: one evening he rereads that story by Chekhov in which two chaste lovers toboggan together on a big sledge, bonded by a murmured declaration of love. He discovers that his memory had greatly modified the plot. For in Chekhov the two lovers do not repeat their ride down a snow-covered slope. In later years the man encounters his former girlfriend and wonders on what whim he had long ago whispered: 'I love you, Nadenka.' The story is called 'A Little Joke', a prank. In Russian, *shutochka*, the same derivation as the name Shutov . . . He pictures Chekhov, settled in a snow-covered *dacha* or in sunny Capri, pen in hand, with a vague, gentle smile, his eyes slightly myopic, as he observes these two characters, seated on their toboggan, coming to life on the page . . . The violent feeling suddenly overcomes Shutov that he will never be a part of the Russian world that is now being reborn within his native land. ('So much the better!' he says to himself.) He will remain to the end in an increasingly despised and indeed, increasingly unknown, past. A period he knows to be indefensible, yet one in which some beings lived who must, at all costs, be rescued from oblivion.

He returns to Russia in mid-September. The home to which Volsky had been sent is located not far from Vyborg, about a hundred miles north of St Petersburg. Shutov had learned of the old man's death while he was still in France, in a telephone conversation with the establishment's head doctor.

This 'home for the elderly' (as it is officially designated) is not the poorhouse he had pictured. Simply, everything there is from another era: the inmates, the staff, the building itself. 'The Soviet era,' thinks Shutov and realizes it may well be the wretched vestiges of those days that enable the old people to have the illusion of not being totally rejected. They die amid a décor they have known during their lifetimes.

What amazes him more is the graveyard. Especially the number of tombs on which the only inscription is either 'u.w.' or 'u.m.' '"Unknown woman", "unknown man",' the attendant explains. 'They're sometimes brought to the home in such a state that they're no longer capable of speech. And there are old people who die in the street, too. Who knows where they've come from . . .'

The graveyard is small, next to an empty church. By climbing onto the front steps overgrown with wild plants, one can make out the dull grey of the Gulf of

Finland . . . That evening Shutov spends a long while walking among the stone slabs covered with golden leaves, reading strange, ancient Christian names. Then he sits down on the steps. This fresh journey of his into Russia, he thinks, is precisely the final section Chekhov recommended cutting in a short story. Which is where the frontier lies between an elegant plunge into fine prose and the rough, patient prose of our lives.

What is most troubling is still this way of summing up a human existence: 'u.w.', 'u.m.' He has made arrangements with a workman to come next day and erect a stone over Volsky's grave bearing his complete name, the date of his birth and that of his death. It had to be done, Shutov tells himself ('the final section') but, nevertheless, will this inscription tell people any more than the notation: 'unknown man'? Perhaps even less.

He gets up, moves towards the exit and suddenly stops. What must be written about is just this: the 'unknown women' and 'unknown men' who loved one another and whose words have remained unvoiced.

Walking along the road that leads towards the home he catches sight of the faintly misty line of the Gulf of Finland.

He has never seen so much of the sky in a single glance before.